Just Fo

ELIZABETH SMITH

Heartline
Books

Published by Heartline Books Limited in 2002

Copyright © Elizabeth Smith 2002

Elizabeth Smith has asserted her rights under the
Copyright, Designs and Patents Act, 1988 to be identified
as the author of this work.

This is a work of fiction. Names and characters are the
product of the author's imagination and any resemblance
to any actual persons, living or dead, is purely
coincidental.

All rights reserved. No part of this publication may be
reproduced, stored in or introduced into a retrieval system
or transmitted by any form, or by any means (electronic,
mechanical, photocopying, recording or otherwise) without
the prior written permission of the publisher. Any person
who takes any unauthorised action in relation to this
publication may be liable to criminal prosecution and
civil claims for damages.

Heartline Books Limited and Heartline Books logo are
trademarks of the publisher.

First published in the United Kingdom in 2002
by Heartline Books Limited.

Heartline Books Limited
PO Box 22598, London W8 7GB

Heartline Books Ltd. Reg No: 03986653

ISBN 1-903867-46-0

Styled by Oxford Designers & Illustrators

Printed and bound in Great Britain by
Cox & Wyman, Reading, Berkshire

ELIZABETH SMITH

ELIZABETH SMITH is an artist and writer who candidly (and gleefully) admits that in order to make time for writing she had to give up cleaning house and cooking!

Together with her husband, Don, she works in the family business in Mississippi, USA, where they design and manufacture a nationally distributed line of ceramic tiles. Elizabeth and Don have also renovated several houses and, along the way, she has discovered some useful talents she didn't know she had!

Elizabeth finds inspiration for her books in 'seemingly ordinary people who, when faced with danger or adversity, are capable of the most extraordinary things.'

Of all the places Elizabeth has visited in the world, Venice is her favourite. She thinks it's the most romantic city anywhere, but also loves its element of mystery…and the breathtaking architecture.

Heartline Books is delighted to offer readers JUST FOR ONE NIGHT by this talented author, whose previous novels have already been enjoyed by women all over the world.

—◆—

Heartline Books – Romance at its best

Call the Heartline Hotline on 0845 6000 504 and order any book you may have missed – you can now pay over the phone by credit or debit card.

Have you visited the Heartline website yet?

If you haven't – and even for those of you who have – it's well worth a trip as we are constantly updating our site.

So log on to www.heartlinebooks.com where you can…

- ♥ Order one or more books – including titles you may have missed – and pay by credit or debit card
- ♥ Check out special offers and events, such as celebrity interviews
- ♥ Find details of our writing classes for aspiring authors
- ♥ Read more about Heartline authors
- ♥ Enter competitions
- ♥ Browse through our catalogue

And much, much more…

In loving memory of my mother, Virginia Ferriter

chapter one

Scurrying from the bathroom into the hall, Amanda leaned over the rail at the top of the stairs and called out. When she failed to get a response, she hurried down the elegant stairway, her bare feet slapping against the worn treads.

'Sam, didn't you hear me calling to you to come in? I don't have any clothes on as you can...' Amanda opened the front door wide, looked up and froze in mid-sentence, her words and thoughts vanquished by a pair of startling blue eyes that glittered expectantly as they locked with hers.

He stood on the porch, his hips thrust slightly forward, his hands hooked into the back pockets of his jeans. Slowly he released the gaze that held hers, but only to let his eyes roam in leisurely inspection down the length of her and back.

'Do you always leave your door unlocked?' he asked. The voice was deep and amused.

His words jarred her into action. She clutched the fabric at her throat with one hand, while her other hand reached for the overlapping folds of her blue cotton robe. Then she checked the sash, making sure it was tightly knotted.

'I'm expecting someone,' she said. 'A man.' As his eyebrows lifted in silent questioning, she hastened to explain. 'It's business.'

He smiled at this, and the fine lines that appeared at the corner of each eye testified to the amount of time he spent outdoors, adding a dimension of ruggedness to his already handsome face.

'I'm sure it is,' he said.

Amanda crossed her arms. 'I don't have to explain

anything to you. I don't even know you.' But she did – the moment he smiled she had recognised him. Right now, the best she could do was hope he didn't remember her.

'I'm Price McCord.'

'Well, how nice for you,' she said, and then shut the door in his face. She waited for the sound of retreating footsteps, but didn't hear any. So she waited a few minutes longer, listening intently for the sound of a departing car. She didn't hear that either. Finally, she opened the door again. As she suspected, he was still standing in her doorway.

'Tell me again who you were expecting,' he said.

'Anyone but you,' she replied with sarcasm.

'Did you really think I would give up and go home that easily?' he asked.

'I was hoping you would surprise me.' Adjusting the damp towel she had wrapped turban-style around her freshly washed hair, she said, 'What do you want?'

'Well for one thing, you could try being nicer.'

'Not a chance. I've had a lousy day.' All afternoon, Amanda had struggled to control her frayed emotions. Confronted with the inability to change her circumstances, and bitterly disappointed at the turn things had taken, she could no longer ignore the reality of her situation. She had failed miserably.

The appearance of Price McCord just made things worse. She should have just bolted the door and left him on the porch until he went away, but old dreams die hard. Instead, she was intrigued by his boldness and found it impossible to ignore the trickle of excitement that started somewhere in the region of her breasts, where her ribs met, and was now working its way downward, gathering momentum as it went.

Adding to this excitement was the possibility that he didn't recognise her. After all, it had been a long time since they had seen one another, and the boy she remembered had now been replaced by a man – a man who radiated an undeniable sexuality.

'I saw your sign by the road,' he said, 'so I came to see the house.' Then, without waiting for a response, he stepped around Amanda and came inside, peering into the large rooms on either side of the central hallway as he went toward the back of the house. Feeling her eyes on him, he turned back to her suddenly, catching her as she openly perused the length of him.

Amanda blushed with a heat that went from her toes to the roots of her hair. What had gotten into her? She had never reacted to any man this way before, and she wished he would wipe that knowing grin off his face. With that thought, she knew what she had been trying to pinpoint since Price McCord first smiled at her – he had the look of a rogue! In another life, he could have been a pirate. It was a look that had haunted women since the beginning of civilisation – the same one that men had used to their advantage for just as long.

'Still like what you see, Amanda?'

Gone was her advantage. He remembered her. 'Go away, Price,' she said, angry at herself for being nearly mesmerised by him.

'But the sign says your house is for sale.'

'It also says "By appointment only", but you must have decided that part didn't apply to you.'

He smiled and stepped closer.

She retreated, only to find her back up against the wall.

His eyes never left hers as he reached out and captured an errant strand of damp hair with his fingertips. Gently, he tucked it into the towel. This done, he turned his hand so his knuckles lightly brushed her temple then lazily moved to her cheek where her skin still glowed rosy from its recent scrubbing. Slowly, he continued his sensual exploration as he ran his index finger over her lips.

The tip of his finger felt abrasive against the smoothness of her full lower lip. Nearly in a trance, Amanda closed her eyes. When he leaned forward, she could feel his warm breath against her face and knew he was about to kiss her. The anticipation made her dizzy.

Distantly, Price registered the sound of a car coming up the driveway. He straightened and stepped back, then in a voice that sent quivers through her he whispered, 'The man you've been waiting for is here.'

From the doorway, Amanda watched as Price left her and went outside to meet Sam Johnson. The two men conversed for several minutes and exchanged business cards. Then the pair parted and Sam called a greeting in her direction as he hurried toward the house.

Absently, Amanda acknowledged the older man's approach, then stepped back to let him enter the house. Sam greeted her, but the sound of his words were lost on her, dissipated in the thick, fragrant afternoon heat. For a few seconds, Price stood in the driveway staring at her. Lingering in the shadows beyond the threshold, she stared back, unwilling and unable to look away. Finally, he turned, and with an easy saunter headed toward his car, while Amanda watched helplessly as the most electrifying man she had ever known got into his car and drove out of her life.

Twenty minutes later, now fully possessed of her senses and fully dressed, Amanda set a glass of iced tea in front of Sam. Then she poured one for herself, carried it to the table, and slid into the chair across from him.

With his narrow face and thinning grey hair, Sam Johnson had always looked the same to Amanda. He had been a family friend for many years, but today the reason for his visit was all business. Earlier in the week, Amanda had asked him to handle the sale of her grandmother's house through his real estate company.

She toyed with her spoon then looked up. 'That man

who was here when you drove up, uh, do you know him?' she asked.

Sam reached into his shirt pocket and pulled out a business card then unfolded his wire-framed glasses. Once he had adjusted the glasses on his nose, he read off the information to Amanda. 'Price McCord. McCord & Company, has an office in downtown Atlanta,' he said. 'I thought you knew him.'

'I do,' she replied. 'That is, I did. He visited the Singletons one summer when he and Bobby were college roommates. He saw the sign.'

'That's what he told me too,' said Sam. 'He said he was out driving and decided to stop on impulse.' Sam paused then frowned at Amanda over the rim of his glasses. 'But the next time someone knocks on your door and wants to see the house, just tell them to call me for an appointment. That's what I'm here for. Better to be safe, especially since you're out here by yourself now. You never know who you're letting in.'

'No, you don't.' *No, indeed.*

Sam drank from his glass, then added more sugar. 'I've put an ad in the paper for Sunday,' he said gently.

Amanda sighed. 'Oh, Sam.'

'We need to get the house sold,' he reminded her. 'The clock is working against us.'

'I had no idea this would be so difficult.'

'You tried, Amanda.'

'I know. I just never thought… Maybe if I had known, I could have changed her mind, or done something different.'

'Your grandmother was a stubborn, independent woman. It was never her intention to leave you in this predicament. She loved you more than anything, you know,' Sam said. Amanda's grandmother, Margaret Hamilton, had been his friend for many years. Like Amanda, he had grieved over her death.

'I know, Sam. If only she had told me…'

But Amanda knew there was no use in rehashing the past. Margaret Hamilton, her judgement clouded by a long and debilitating illness, had mortgaged her beautiful old house. Not once, but twice. It wasn't until after her death that Amanda found out about the second mortgage, taken out only weeks before her death. When added together, the payments were more than Amanda could handle.

For the past six months she had struggled, falling further behind each month. Her only hope of keeping the house was to get a new mortgage – one that combined the old debt and spread the repayment out over a longer period. But every bank she had approached refused to make the loan, citing every reason but the real one – she was young, single and self-employed, the latter a choice she had made so that she could work at home and care for Margaret at the same time.

Sam had offered to help her out, more than once, but Amanda had refused. One of these days he would need the money he had put away for his retirement, in spite of his protest to the contrary.

Sam leaned back in his chair. 'Look Amanda, you've got your whole life ahead of you. Maybe later you'll see this in a different light.'

'Oh Sam, I don't know.' Even though her heart was heavy, she forced herself to smile at him. Sam was the kindest man she knew, and right now he was the only person in the world she could count on. 'I'll do my best to see this as a new beginning.'

Early on Saturday morning, Amanda carried her coffee to the study, then went to the window as she did most mornings to watch the birds at play. Today their unremarkable brown colour was relieved by the vivid scarlet of several cardinals as they gathered in the shade of the huge oak tree.

The study had always been her favourite room, and it was here that she did most of her work. Her drawing board was centred in front of the window that faced south. Her paints and other supplies were there too, in a small metal cabinet. Bookshelves, filled with beautiful old books and a variety of items Margaret had collected over the years, lined the rest of the room. To her right was her computer, along with reference books and her collection of books on art.

At the drawing board, Amanda pulled up her stool and studied the colourful illustrations she had completed the previous day. Then, reaching for a clean sheet of paper, she took her pencil and began to sketch. She was an accomplished artist, a talent that seemingly came from out of the blue, since no one in the family that Margaret could remember had ever exhibited even a passing interest in art. Amanda illustrated children's books, and her work was always in demand. By most standards, her freelance business paid well – just not well enough, or regularly enough, to satisfy any of the banks she had approached.

An hour later, she was deeply immersed in her work when she was startled by a knock at the door. She jumped, hitting her knee against the small cabinet that held her supplies and the cup she had just refilled. The dark liquid sloshed over the rim, spreading over the cabinet top. 'Damn,' she muttered as she reached for a roll of paper towels, hoping that it hadn't ruined anything.

Sam had told her he would always call ahead of time whenever a prospective buyer wanted to see the house, but maybe he had forgotten. Amanda stopped for a moment to check her appearance in the hall mirror, wiping a pencil smudge off her face. Then she tucked her shirt into her denim skirt.

When she opened the door, she was stunned. Standing there was Price McCord. Again. All heart-stopping six feet of him. With his arms propped on either side, he seemed to fill the doorway and tower over her. She wished she could say that she hadn't thought of him during the two days since he had first appeared at her door, but she had. More than she cared to admit – more than she should have!

She wished he would say something, anything. But Price just stared at her in the strangest way, like he was seeing her for the first time. Uncomfortable with this intense scrutiny, Amanda reached up to tuck her hair behind her right ear. It was a nervous gesture, something she did when she was feeling self-conscious, like she was now.

'I made an appointment,' he said finally, as he stepped forward, a slight frown on his face as if he were irritated at himself for being here, and maybe feeling a little foolish.

Amanda stepped back, pulling the door she still grasped back against the wall. But this time, his spectacular looks took a back seat to her temper. 'I don't remember inviting you in,' she snapped, 'but that doesn't seem to bother you at all, does it?'

'This is not a social call, Amanda. You do have a "For Sale" sign up, and this time I followed the rules.'

'Do you think that sign means that I have to open my house to anyone who comes along?'

'But I'm not just anyone, am I?' Price asked, giving her one of his most charming smiles.

When she failed to return his smile, Price continued. 'Sam warned me that you might not be too hospitable if he didn't call you ahead of time,' he said, looking away into the living room, 'but I told him not to bother.'

Amanda ignored that and asked, 'You talked to Sam about the house? Why?'

'I might buy it – if I like what I see,' Price replied. 'Now since Sam's not here, will you show me around?'

'We can wait for him.' Amanda crossed her arms and stubbornly stood her ground.

'Could be a problem. Especially since I told him there was no reason for him to drive all the way out here.'

'You've got a lot of nerve, Price.'

'It usually gets me what I want. Now, will you show me the house, or do I have to call poor old Sam to come out on a hot day like today?'

Amanda turned and muttered something in reply. Her voice was low, but Price could have sworn she called him a bully.

She began the tour in the study, then she led him back into the hall and into the living room and the dining room. Each of these rooms were large, with high ceilings and fireplaces. Reluctantly, she pointed out what she considered to be the best features of each room, realising that the more attractive she made the house sound, the sooner it would sell. But not to Price McCord.

Price followed her through the house taking careful note of everything about her that had been hidden by her robe on his first visit, and decided that Amanda Hamilton had grown up nicely. Among other things, he was acutely aware of the swing of her hips in the short denim skirt as she went from one room to the next. And he couldn't help but note how the sunlight bounced off her shoulder-length hair, turning strands of shiny brown to red and gold. When she stopped and turned toward him, he measured her with his eyes and knew that the top of her head would tuck nicely under his chin.

When he realised where his thoughts were leading, he stopped, annoyed with himself. There were more than enough attractive women around to satisfy his needs. He didn't need to bother with this one. Besides, she was too young. But something about her tugged at him. He had felt it the other day, then again today.

Readjusting his attention, Price focused on the interior details of the house. Certainly it had harboured generations whose lives had been touched by happiness, sadness, war, poverty and prosperity. With so much family history, it was a shame to part with it. Price wondered what had prompted Amanda to put the house up for sale.

'How long has this house been in your family?'

She turned to face him. Her anxiety over his scrutiny disappeared. This beautiful home, which was referred to by nearly everyone who lived in the area as the Hamilton-Sperry house, was a source of pride to her. 'Over one-hundred-and-forty years,' she answered. 'It was built by Edward Hamilton for his bride, Eugenia Sperry, just before the Civil War. It was one of the few homes around here to survive the war, probably because it's a little off the beaten path. It is beautiful, isn't it?' asked Amanda, her eyes shining.

'Yes, it is,' answered Price truthfully. It was obvious that she loved this house. So why was she selling it?

'Come on,' she said quickly. 'I'll show you upstairs.'

The entire house was surprisingly light and airy, probably due to the colours Amanda had used; several shades of ivory along with white and pale blue. Here and there were a few chosen pieces in terracotta and apricot. Amanda had added the touch of an artist to an interior that could just as easily have been dark and uninspired; j18
decorating the house with all the old-fashioned things that were supposed to be there.

Price was amazed. This was exactly the kind of warm, comfortable feeling he had wanted Caroline to create at Cumberland River instead of the too-perfect model homes he had ended up with. Granted, Caroline's impeccable taste had prevailed, but the overall result had lacked warmth.

Amanda concluded the tour in the smallest bedroom

that overlooked several outbuildings at the back of the house. It was her bedroom, the one she had chosen when she had come to stay with Margaret.

'Well, now you've seen everything,' she said, flustered by his nearness. His presence in her room seemed to invade her privacy. Suddenly breathless, she whirled around quickly, intending to lead him out into the hall, but instead she ran right into the solid expanse of his chest. She stumbled, taking a faltering step backward.

He caught her by the arms.

At his touch, she felt as if she had been running for miles, her breath was coming in uneven spurts, her temperature rising, his hands heating her flesh. Her heart was beating a rapid cadence, but all she could do was stand there with her eyes fixed on the third button of his shirt.

Slowly, he lifted one hand and brought it, fingers outstretched, under her chin to lightly guide her face upward. 'Look at me, Amanda,' he said in a slow, sensuous drawl.

Unable to resist, she raised her soft brown eyes as he commanded.

Intently he studied her eyes, her small straight nose, and her perfectly shaped mouth. Slowly, he moved his fingers from beneath her chin and, as he had on his previous visit, he ran his index finger over her full lower lip. His gaze lingered there, and she responded by parting her lips slightly. This was the response he had wanted, and indeed a response he had got many times before with other women. But hers was natural, not coyly calculated to elicit an answering response from him.

Was she truly what she appeared to be? Instinctively, he knew that there was a depth and an honesty here that he rarely encountered in the women he knew. Or was it that he just never got to know them well enough? Irrationally and unexpectedly, he had been sexually attracted to Amanda from the first moment she had opened her door to him. Suddenly, he realised he hadn't felt this way about anyone for a long time. Returning his attention to her upturned face, he leaned closer and lowered his lips to hers.

Amanda drew in her breath sharply. She had wanted him to do this from the first moment she had seen him, and now that he had, she had no idea what to do. His lips were warm and firm, his tongue lightly probing. At odds was the weakness she felt in her arms and legs and the excitement building within her, she raised her arms and wrapped them around his neck.

Price savoured the sweetness of her mouth as he explored its recesses. Somewhere far off, his mind registered the thought that Amanda kissed as though she hadn't been kissed in a very long time. She seemed hesitant and unsure of what to do next. Well, he knew exactly what to do next. Moving his hands slowly up and down her back, he deepened their kiss.

Dimly, she felt his hands move from her back to her waist, and from there they began to move slowly upward. She gasped inwardly when she felt the palms of his hands touch the soft rounded sides of her breasts.

She was torn between the need to stop this now before it became more, and the almost overwhelming desire to have him do this and much, much more! She turned her head quickly to break their kiss and then stood silently, breathlessly trying to regain her composure. Suddenly embarrassed, she pushed by him, rushed down the stairs and went out to the porch.

She needed some room to breathe, to gather her composure. It was just a kiss, she thought, the kiss she had yearned for for years. But now she was grown and she knew better than to place any importance on a kiss from a man like this. He was only playing with her.

Price followed her outside and stood behind her. Then

he gently wrapped his arms around her. With his lips so close to her ear that she could feel his warm breath, he whispered, 'Was that your bedroom?'

She nodded.

'Pretty,' he murmured, 'and soft – like you. Didn't you like it?'

'The bedroom?' she asked, deliberately choosing to misunderstand him. 'Of course I like it.'

'Quit playing games, Amanda,' he said. Then he turned her around so that she faced him. 'This is what I meant.' Again he dipped his head and kissed her.

It was just like the one before, only better. And longer. And absolutely incredible. Suddenly she pulled away, breaking all contact.

'Look at me,' Price commanded softly.

But Amanda had her eyes trained on his powerful forearms, studying them as if she hoped to memorise the look and feel of them.

'I didn't mean to upset you,' he said gently.

'You didn't,' she said. 'I'm just not good at…'

'You were fine,' he said.

She worried that her inexperienced kiss had given her away. She was sure he was just trying to be nice to her, to ease an awkward moment. It only made things worse. 'I…I'm not very good at this,' she said.

Her candour startled Price. He grinned, then before she could see his amusement, he reached to tilt her chin once more, forcing her eyes to meet his. 'What you need is more practice.'

A look of apprehension crossed Amanda's face.

Price grinned then planted another kiss on her lips, this one quick and playful. 'But we can work on that another time,' he said teasingly as he turned away and headed toward his car.

chapter two

Amanda glanced at her watch and decided to walk the short distance to the café where she was meeting Joan for lunch. In spite of her problems, her step was bouncy and her attitude positive. When she arrived, she anxiously scanned the midday crowd and spotted her friend at a table on the far side of the restaurant. With her wild, flaming red hair, it was always easy to find Joan Cunningham in a crowd.

'You certainly look happy today,' said Joan when Amanda had joined her.

Amanda sank into the chair opposite her. 'I am,' she answered. 'I just posted "Rosie's New Family" a full week ahead of schedule, and this morning I had an email from the editor telling me that they have several other books for me to illustrate.' Amanda's artwork was always beautiful, imaginative, well-executed and exactly what she and the editor had decided upon. 'It's a great way to wind up the week. How are you doing?'

Joan leaned forward. 'Amanda, the most exciting thing has happened – I've met a new man.'

Amanda threw her head back and laughed. Her eyes were full of mischief. 'Another one?' she asked with mock surprise. 'I can't wait to hear all about his many charms.'

Joan took Amanda's teasing in stride. The new men in Joan's life were the stuff legends were made of. 'This one is different,' she said.

'You say that about every man you meet,' replied Amanda as the waiter brought their iced tea.

Secretly Amanda wished she knew how to attract men that easily. Joan evidently had this thing, this appeal that she lacked. Since college, Joan had done her best to tutor Amanda on how to capitalise on her looks, not that there was anything wrong with the way she looked. It was just that she didn't know how to use what she had. Whenever an opportunity arose with the opposite sex, it was as if she automatically took a mental step back, becoming aloof while her body language practically screamed 'hands off'. Men did not hang around after that. The worst part was that she wasn't even aware of what she had done until it was too late. Had she done that with Price McCord? If she had, it didn't seem to bother him.

Today her dark shiny hair was set off by the pale pink blouse she wore with her suit. Maybe that was the major difference between the two friends right there – the reason Joan never lacked male attention. It all came down to the packaging, Amanda decided. Joan would have worn that suit without a blouse and before she left the restaurant today she would have a date for tonight. Amanda would have felt naked.

'No,' said Joan, shaking her head. 'This time I really mean it. He's not like anyone else I've dated.'

'What makes this one different?'

'He's...' Joan shrugged her shoulders and raised her hands palms upward, searching for the right words. 'Scholarly and smart,' Joan concluded.

'And incredibly sexy, no doubt,' added Amanda.

'No, well, yeah,' said Joan. 'That's the funny part. There's something about him, but he's not handsome. He's the kind who looks calm and in control on the outside, but I just know that if I ever got him out of his glasses and his boxers and into bed, he'd be a sex machine.'

Amanda laughed. 'Here we go again.'

'No,' said Joan. 'I really mean it. It sounds corny, but he's a gentleman. And I think he really likes me as a person. I'm just speculating on the sex part. We haven't progressed that far.'

Amanda raised an eyebrow at this. How she and Joan had remained friends was a miracle. Their values were so different and, most of the time, Amanda had to work hard not to be judgemental. To Joan, sex was a part of the dating ritual. Amanda's opposing views on sex, and the proper time for it, was the only discordant note in their friendship.

'Where did you meet this guy?' asked Amanda.

'He moved into my apartment building a few weeks ago. He's an electrical engineer.'

'One of the dull boys,' quipped Amanda.

'Not really,' said Joan as she stirred her iced tea. 'He's charming and witty in a quiet way. And I find the fact that he hasn't tried to get me into bed very intriguing.'

'He must want to drive you crazy.'

Joan grinned. 'I think so, but I'm not sure if it's intentional or just the way he is.'

It was only when the waiter brought their lunch that Amanda sat back and let her eyes wander over the crowd then back again to a couple making their way to a table across the room. With a start, she realised that the man was Price McCord. He looked so different in a suit and tie, powerful and in control. Then she saw the woman he was with, and her buoyant mood vanished. The woman was everything she wasn't. In short, she was a knockout.

'What's wrong?' asked Joan. 'You look like you've seen a ghost.'

'I have,' answered Amanda. 'But he looks a lot different than he did the last time I saw him. Don't look now, but see that tall, dark-haired man? Over there?' Amanda nodded her head in the general direction.

As usually happens when people preface a sentence with 'Don't look now', Joan immediately reached into her purse for her glasses and, putting them on, she began a rather obvious search for the man Amanda had just described. Finding him, she said, 'Wow, you know him?'

Amanda nodded, hoping that she would be able to leave the restaurant without being seen.

Joan pressed for details. 'Where did you find a man like that?'

'I didn't exactly find him,' answered Amanda wryly. 'He found me. I mean, he found my house.' Amanda repeated the story of her meeting with Price and the fact that they had met before. 'I was stunned to see him at my door after all these years. Just look at him.'

Joan turned once more to do just that.

'But that's not all,' added Amanda. 'Two days later, he came back to the house again.' Amanda looked across the restaurant and sighed. 'I must have been hallucinating, thinking that he might have come back a second time because of me. Just look at the woman he's with.'

Price's companion appeared to be about the same age as Amanda. She was tall and slender with straight, chin-length auburn hair that framed her face. With her flawlessly applied make-up, and her pale-grey tailored dress, she looked like she had just stepped from the pages of the latest fashion magazine.

With a sinking feeling, Amanda knew now that Price had kissed her for fun. He wasn't interested in her. When he told he had come to see the house, she should have believed him.

'She's definitely an attention-getter,' agreed Joan, 'and Price McCord is absolutely gorgeous.'

'And definitely out of my league,' said Amanda in a small, unsure voice. *Some things never change.*

'He's not only handsome,' Joan said lightly as she deliberately tried to brighten the tone of their conversation, 'he's sexy. He could even be dangerous and those are the best kind. But he's not out of your league. Amanda. If you don't develop some self-confidence along with a decent social life, I'm afraid you're going to wind up an old maid,' Joan said teasingly. 'You won't even have any memories to keep you warm on cold nights. At least I'll have memories,' Joan said with a smug grin.

With a fork full of salad suspended in mid-air, Amanda inquired more sharply than she intended, 'And at what age do I become an old maid? Besides, Joan, I would hardly call your affairs memorable. Hopping in to bed on the first date is not something to brag about.'

As friends, Joan and Amanda were a strange combination. They were opposites in almost everything, and yet this friendship had endured since college.

Realising that she had touched a nerve, Joan said, 'I was just teasing about that, Amanda. I didn't mean it literally. But you do need to put yourself in a position to meet more men. You not only work at home, but you practically live in the country. When was the last time you went out on a date?'

'I don't remember,' said Amanda. It was true. She couldn't remember. So much had happened. Had it been last summer or the summer before?

'My point exactly. Maybe you should move out of that mausoleum,' said Joan.

'I am.'

'What?'

'I am,' repeated Amanda. 'I've put "the mausoleum" up for sale and, as soon as I have a buyer, I'm moving.'

'That's wonderful,' cried Joan, aware of the difficult time Amanda had been having since Margaret's death. 'That's a really positive first step.'

'No, it's not.'

'It will be. You just wait.'

All during lunch, Joan kept glancing in Price's direction. When they were nearly finished, she said, 'Amanda, why don't you go over and say hello. That way you can get a closer look at the woman he's with – you know, size up the competition.'

Amanda frowned. 'I got a look at her. What I saw wasn't good, and there is no competition – at least not for her.'

'Maybe it's just a business lunch,' said Joan.

'Not with my luck. Come on,' Amanda mumbled. 'Let's hurry and get out of here. Chances are about a million-to-one that Price McCord will notice me, but if he did, then I'd have to speak to him.'

Amanda's spirits had soared when she had first seen him, then plummeted when she had noticed the woman he was with. Gone was any hope that he could possibly be interested in her. For an instant, she was fifteen again, hoping he would notice her, and when he did it was a disaster. She had nearly fallen, tripped over her own feet, then grabbed at his arm to steady herself. He had laughed – it was funny – but she had been mortified.

But this was real life, not the daydreams she had about him when she was a teenager, and definitely not the fantasy she had been having for the past several days. In this setting, Price looked even more powerful, if that was possible, like a man who always got what he wanted, like a man who already had everything he wanted.

'I'm definitely not his style,' Amanda said wistfully to Joan as they prepared to leave the restaurant. But in spite of her declaration, she desperately wished she was.

She couldn't get him off her mind. Contrary to the sensible advice she had given herself to forget about Price, Amanda still secretly hoped she would see him again. She was fascinated by him, just as she had been the summer when she'd first met him. But she had been a child then, a shy young girl overcome by her first real crush. And he was in college, nearly a man. Even though she was a woman now, she was still vulnerable when it came to Price McCord.

She had never been around a man who had had such an effect on her. She suspected he was a very complex man. Certainly he was the most blatantly sensual man she had ever encountered, and it was this that disturbed and fascinated her the most.

Early the following Monday morning, Sam Johnson had just unlocked the door to his real estate office when he heard the phone ringing. He glanced at the clock, laid his worn briefcase on the desk and answered the phone.

'Sam, this is Price McCord. I'm calling about Amanda Hamilton's house.'

'What did you think of it?' asked Sam in a neutral voice.

'I'd like to have it, Sam,' Price answered. 'But first I want to send out a few people to check it over. Given the age of the house, it's important to determine if it's structurally sound.'

'Of course.'

'If this inspection is satisfactory,' said Price, 'you can draw up a contract.'

'What is your offer, Price?' asked Sam.

'That depends. Why is she selling the place?'

Sam hesitated. He had no intention of divulging Amanda's financial problems, but he had to give Price an answer that was as honest as possible. 'It's just too large a house for one person now that Margaret Hamilton has passed away. Amanda wants to move into town.'

'Was Margaret Hamilton her mother?' inquired Price.

'Grandmother,' answered Sam. 'She died about six months ago.'

'I see.' Silently, Price surmised that Amanda needed the money. It was the only acceptable reason for selling such a magnificent home. 'If the house is sound, I'll pay the full asking price. By the way,' continued Price casually, 'who's the mortgage holder?'

Since this was such an ordinary question, and one that Sam was asked frequently during real estate transactions, he responded without a second thought. 'First Security Trust.' Just as the words left his mouth, Sam realised his mistake. With that one piece of information, he might as well have spilled his guts about Amanda's finances. A house the calibre and age of the Hamilton-Sperry house would never be mortgaged except under the most extreme circumstances. Sam, who had always considered himself a shrewd and knowledgeable negotiator, had just been outmanoeuvred.

'How bad?' asked Price.

Sam, deciding there was no way out of this, answered truthfully. 'Bad. Amanda's tried everything to try to hold on to the house. Her grandmother's illness nearly wiped both of them out. Margaret was the one who mortgaged the place without telling Amanda. After she died, Amanda found out there was a second mortgage also. She's been fighting this ever since. It's just more debt than she can handle. Unfortunately, when she tried to get new financing, she was turned down.'

'Go ahead and set up an appointment for my people to go through the house late tomorrow afternoon, but Sam, I don't want her to know I'm the buyer. Not just yet.'

'What are you going to do with the house?' asked Sam curiously.

Financially, Price was secure but he lived like a gypsy, travelling frequently and using his apartment only to shower, change clothes, and occasionally sleep. Maybe the house represented stability and a sense of belonging. But because he was an architect and builder, he had to admit that the Hamilton-Sperry house, with its fifty acres of land and its proximity to Atlanta, might have the potential for development.

Plans were already on the drawing board and he was ready to go with them just as soon as he acquired the right plot of land. Since the completion of Cumberland River, which had been wildly successful and profitable even beyond his expectations, all of his attempts to acquire land to build on had ended in frustration. Many of the plots he had hoped to acquire were part of large estates held either by feuding heirs or hopelessly entangled in litigation. Others, when subjected to the idiosyncrasies and restrictions of local city and county governments, made development unadvisable.

Price remembered the first time he had seen Amanda's house during a summer visit with the Singletons. He had been in college then, and even after all these years he remembered the feeling – as if he had stepped back in time. The pale pink brick, faded by exposure to the elements for over a century-and-a-half, had softened and blurred the lines of the house. On either side of the doorway, long windows framed by faded moss-green shutters soared from floor to ceiling, while hundreds of paned glass panels reflected the dancing images of the majestic trees that surrounded the house. Tall white columns climbed toward the sky.

The scene had had an ethereal quality and, for just a fleeting moment, Price wondered if he had imagined it all. But he never forgot the sweet odour of the wild honeysuckle that surrounded him that day. It was also the first time he saw Amanda Hamilton.

'It's a beautiful place, Sam,' said Price. 'And it has great potential for someone who has the resources to restore it. I'm not really sure what I'll do with it.' It was as honest an answer as he could give.

The decision to buy had been easy, but the truth was that he really didn't know what his motives were. The home had a feeling of timelessness even though its design was firmly rooted in another century. There was something about it that tugged at him. It offered a sense of permanence and peace, two things that were missing from his life.

The shrill ring of the phone startled Amanda out of her reverie.

'Amanda, this is Sam. I've got some people who want to look at the house late tomorrow afternoon.'

'Certainly. I'll arrange to be away while you're showing it.' As she hung up a few minutes later, the realisation that she was actually going to sell the house hit her. It was only a matter of time now before someone would make an offer. Once again, Amanda tried to imagine the kind of people who would soon be living here. Maybe a family, she thought. The house would be perfect for children.

But all she could visualise was the same scene she had pictured for so many years. She pictured herself in her studio, not the makeshift studio in the study, but the new light-filled studio with lots of windows that had been added to the back of the house. At her feet, a small child was playing quietly.

Amanda sighed, shaking her head sadly. Not only would she be leaving this house soon, but she couldn't begin to hope to make her dream come true. She was twenty-five-years-old and there was not a single prospect on her horizon who could possibly fill the role of perfect husband and father to her perfect child.

Tuesday was bright and sunny. It would be another hot day, nothing unusual for this time of year. Over a late breakfast, Amanda contemplated how she would spend her day and what she would do this afternoon while Sam was showing the house. With her last project completed and the others not yet arrived, she actually had the luxury of a day all to herself. Idly, she wondered how Price spent his days off. *Probably in bed with that woman he was with at lunch*, she thought.

After an hour she was no closer to deciding how she was going to spend the afternoon while Sam was showing the house, so she decided instead to take a shower.

She had just finished rinsing her hair when she heard the phone ring. 'It's probably Joan,' she muttered. Joan always called when she was in the shower. Grabbing the nearest towel, Amanda stepped out and ran dripping into the bedroom. It wouldn't do any good not to answer the phone. Joan would just keep calling.

She struggled to hold the towel around her and at the same time get the phone to her ear. Dispensing with the preliminaries, she blurted, 'Why is it that whenever you think of me, I'm stark naked and dripping wet?'

The pause at the other end told Amanda that this was definitely not Joan. She closed her eyes. *Oh damn, who is it?* She opened her mouth to ask just as a deep voice chuckled.

'Actually, I only imagine you naked. I hadn't even considered dripping wet.' Amanda's eyes flew open and her whole body blushed as she recognised Price McCord's voice. She struggled valiantly for a witty reply, but none was forthcoming.

'Amanda?'

'What?'

'Are you blushing again?'

'No, I'm cold and I'm standing in a puddle of water.'

'I'll pick you up at four this afternoon. We'll go for a drive then stop somewhere for dinner later.'

'Oh.'

Price was perplexed. He had asked many women to have dinner with him, but he had never had such a lukewarm reply. He had no way of knowing that Amanda was nearly speechless.

'Is that a yes?' he asked after a prolonged silence.

She smiled into the phone. 'Yes, yes, it is.'
'Good. I'll see you then. Oh, and one other thing, dress casual. What you're wearing right now would be perfect.'

chapter three

By the time Price arrived, Amanda had put on, then discarded, three different outfits. Finally she had settled on a sleeveless yellow linen top and matching long skirt. To that she added sandals.

'Not exactly what I requested,' he said, grinning as he looked her over, 'but very pretty.' The look in his blue eyes was assessing.

Amanda blushed at his reference to their phone conversation earlier that day, then desperately wished she could be more like Joan. Why did she have to be so uptight about everything? Why couldn't she just relax and enjoy going to dinner with a great looking guy and not worry about what the rest of the evening would bring? The answer was simple – because it wasn't her style. But tonight she would try.

It was a perfect evening for a drive in the country, and so far Amanda and Price had been polite to one another. The conversation had been light, but each was aware of the strong attraction between them.

Amanda's uncertainty manifested itself as shyness. Her feelings about seeing him again were mixed. On one hand she was excited, on the other, skittish and ready to retreat from his compelling masculinity. It was as if after attracting a man like Price, she had no idea what to do about him, or with him. All he had to do was to look at her in that certain way of his and she would begin to feel all hot. And twitchy. In places where she shouldn't!

In the car, she kept glancing over at him, acutely aware of his nearness. Today he was wearing a white knit shirt with a light blue collar which accentuated his dark good looks. His coppery tan made his eyes appear even bluer. They rode in silence for a while and Amanda was surprised when she realised that they were approaching the motorway that would take them into Atlanta. The route he had chosen had taken them through the countryside on winding back roads.

Soon they arrived at a small Italian restaurant nestled in a modest older neighbourhood. Many of the shops and homes, which had been built in the twenties and thirties, were undergoing renovation. The area was a curious mix of dingy and trendy. But once they were seated and had been served, Amanda could see why Price liked this place. It was intimate and charming and the food was delicious.

'Do you ever see the Singletons?' Price asked.

'Once in a while. The last time was when I was in a shop a few months ago. Mrs Singleton said Bobby still lives in North Carolina, in Charlotte. Do you keep in touch with him?'

'I was in Charlotte on business about six months ago. We had lunch. He's doing well. Who in the world would have ever thought that Bobby would end up as an insurance agent? All he wanted to do in college was party. But he said all that stopped when he met Mary Ellen. Now they have two children and another on the way. Bobby showed me pictures. Cute kids.'

'Do you like kids?' Amanda asked, then wished she hadn't. Her question had been intended to be conversational, but as soon as he answered, she knew it was not a subject he wanted to pursue.

'Yeah, as long as they're someone else's,' Price answered sharply. After a few minutes he asked, 'Amanda, do you remember that summer? How much fun we all had?'

Remember? She wished she could forget it. 'I did some really stupid things, childish things,' she said.

Price grinned. 'You had help. Bobby's little sister was responsible for most of the mischief.'

Amanda giggled. 'But I was a willing accomplice and a faithful follower. My only defence was that I was fifteen.' *And I had such a crush on you.* 'But in case you haven't noticed, I've changed since then.'

'I've noticed, and it's a great improvement.'

She couldn't help but laugh. It was true. At fifteen she had been small and skinny, and her inquisitive brown eyes, peering from beneath her fringe, seemed to dominate her delicate face.

'Well, you didn't ask, but you've changed too,' she said.

'Really?' He leaned forward with interest. 'Am I better looking?'

Amanda ignored his question. 'I didn't say you had improved, Price. I only said you had changed.'

This time it was Price's turn to laugh, and for the remainder of the meal the light banter continued.

Later they left the restaurant and walking hand-in-hand down the street, they peered in the windows of the shops. When they reached the corner Amanda turned, thinking they were about to retrace their steps toward the car. But instead of following her lead, Price stopped and pulled her to him. He made no move to put his arms around her. Holding only her hand in his, he leaned toward her. His kiss was slow and lazy.

The urge to protest, which stemmed from Amanda's opinion that public displays of affection, such as this one, were in bad taste, could wait. There was nothing bad about this – nothing at all.

'You have to stop this,' she said breathlessly after a few minutes.

'What?' he asked.

'This kissing. You can't keep kissing me like this.'

He grinned. 'Didn't you like it?'

'Well, yes, and that's the problem,' she said. 'I liked it a lot.'

'Amanda, I really don't see…'

'I know you don't, Price. Could...could we just go now?' *Before things get any worse.*

'Whatever you want.' His reply was curt.

How could she make him understand what he did to her every time he kissed her? All kinds of crazy things happened inside her heart and in her head. And he made her hope – that was the worst – that he could love her the way she had once loved him. But Amanda knew that would never happen. Men like Price McCord didn't fall in love with someone as ordinary as she. They could do better, and usually did. And, if by chance they showed any interest at all, it was usually just a way to fill the time until someone better came along.

When they were in the car Price asked, 'What's bothering you, Amanda?'

'You,' she answered honestly.

Price formed a silent 'O' with his lips and waited for her to continue.

'I know you, but I don't know anything about you.' Rushing on in a breathless voice as though what she had to say had to be said then or she would never again have the courage, Amanda continued, 'And I don't know what you want from me.'

Price looked away from her toward the road. His jaw tightened, and his grip on the steering wheel intensified. Silence settled around them like a heavy fog. He drove on until he found a turn-off. It was barely wide enough to accommodate the car and was covered by overhanging branches. Slowly, he unfolded his hands from the wheel and shifted in his seat so that he was looking directly at her. He continued to study her while she darted small glances at him from beneath her lowered lashes.

Slowly and deliberately, Price reached out to her, pulling her toward him. Lightly, he ran one hand over her hair, briefly touched it with his lips, then moved down to her temple before finding her soft mouth. 'What I want is you, Amanda,' he whispered. And without hesitation his lips captured hers again, this time with urgency.

Amanda was caught between her body's response to his kiss and her mind's warnings. The battle between passion and reason escalated.

Price continued his onslaught with his warm lips, probing tongue, and the clever hands that had deftly unbuttoned her blouse and were now cupping her breasts, causing them to ache for more of his touch. His mouth moved from her lips to the hollow of her throat, then down to the rise of her breast. She tried to speak, but her words were cut off, as his lips once more reclaimed hers.

He pulled away slightly, his voice low and hoarse and urgent. 'I want to take you somewhere right now. I want to make love to you.'

As his words penetrated her clouded mind, she jerked away from him, shaken by his blunt declaration. She looked down and, for the first time, realised her state of undress. Frantically she clutched at her open blouse, as if by doing so she could regain her composure. And her sanity. He was bad for her, and she felt ashamed of her weakness for him, her pathetic need to be loved.

Price leaned back, resting his head against the door. He said nothing, but his mouth formed a grim line of displeasure. A pulse beat heavily in his neck. He appeared to be in control, but in fact his body was far from it. He hadn't felt desire this raw and this urgent for a long time.

'Is that why you keep coming back to see me, Price? Am I just different enough to provide you with a couple of hours of amusement before you move on to your next challenge? Just how naïve do you think I am?' Amanda was struggling to button her blouse, but her eyes had filled with tears of humiliation that she could have been so foolish to think for even a moment that he might have cared for her.

'Stop, Amanda,' he said harshly as he reached over and pushed her hands away. Slowly he began to button her blouse. 'I don't think you're naïve. I won't tell you things I don't mean and I won't make any promises. I want to make love to you. There's nothing wrong with that. You're not as experienced as some of the women I've known, but there's a remedy for that.'

Amanda inhaled raggedly, as she watched his hands work the buttons of her blouse. 'And I suppose you've known a lot of women?'

Price's head jerked up. Was she serious? Maybe she wasn't one of those women who maintained an air of innocence long after it was gone. Maybe she really was sexually inexperienced. It was obvious that this was no act she was putting on for his benefit. He needed to have his head examined for even being interested in someone like her. 'Amanda, just how experienced are you, sexually I mean?'

She looked at him as if he had just asked her a question in a language she didn't understand. 'I beg your pardon?'

'You heard me. How much experience? How many relationships?'

'That's none of your business. I think this whole evening is a lot more than I bargained for, Price. Please take me home and we'll just forget all about this.'

'How many lovers, Amanda?' he continued. 'One? Two? Maybe in college?'

'I have no intention of answering you. Let's just say that I've had enough experience with men to know that you and I don't want the same things. I know that I want a lot more than just a night of casual sex; I want it to mean something.'

Price was silent for a few moments then slowly straightened and reached to turn the key in the ignition. 'They should be finished with your house now,' he said tersely.

Amanda jerked her head toward him. 'How do you know about my house?'

'Because it's my people who are inspecting it. I'm buying your house. Sam will have the papers ready for me to sign in the morning, providing that the inspection report is satisfactory. He'll have a contract and earnest money in hand before noon tomorrow.'

Amanda was stunned. Vaguely she remembered that he had told her to consider him a potential buyer, but she never took him seriously. Suddenly, she realised why he had made so many visits. Price McCord had succeeded in making a fool out of her in more ways than one.

She sat up very straight and folded her hands in her lap. 'Now that you've decided to buy the house, there won't be any reason for us to see each other again, except at the closing.'

'You're absolutely right,' he replied. 'And if you're ever ready for an adult relationship, you know where to find me. I won't bother you again, Amanda.'

They drove back to the house in silence. When he pulled into the drive she grabbed her bag and hurried from the car as fast as she could. He watched her as she ran up the stairs and into the house.

It was only when she was safely in her room that the tears came, along with the realisation that she was terribly lonely and afraid of taking a chance with this man. She thought about Price and the feelings he aroused in her. Maybe she would never be ready for a relationship of that intensity. Passions of the magnitude that she had experienced with him just didn't fit with his 'no strings' type of encounter. She would want more from a man. Much more.

The next morning, Amanda's reflection stared back at her. Her face and her eyes were puffy from crying and she looked rotten. She felt rotten. When the phone rang, she hesitated then reached for it.

'Amanda? I have great news. We have a buyer for the house. I've been selling real estate a long time, but I don't think I've ever got a contract this fast.'

Amanda managed to murmur an appropriate reply. Then, because she knew it was expected of her, she asked the question she dreaded. 'Who is the buyer?'

'Price McCord,' Sam answered.

'I see,' said Amanda with a sinking heart. Price had done exactly what he had said he was going to do.

'I'm sorry, Sam. I know you're excited about selling the house so quickly, and I should be relieved. At least now I'll know exactly when I'll have to move. It's just that it's going to happen sooner than I anticipated.' If Sam thought she sounded strange, she hoped he would attribute it to the news he had for her. He couldn't expect her to share his enthusiasm under the circumstances.

'Price will be in to sign the contract today before noon, then as soon as we're done here I'll bring it out for you to sign, accepting his offer. Of course, it's more or less a formality. He's offering the full asking price.'

Amanda spent the rest of the day wavering between relief that this gut-wrenching ordeal of selling the house was soon to be over, and resentment that Price McCord was the buyer. How could she think of all the happy years she had spent here without thinking of him? She wanted to call Sam and tell him that no matter how much Price was offering, she would never sell her beloved home to him. But to do that would be foolish. She couldn't wait for another offer. Time was running out and the shameful spectre of foreclosure was never far from her thoughts.

Price had spent the last several days trying to analyse his behaviour that evening with Amanda. She had succeeded in angering him, something he didn't let happen often. But even now, he couldn't keep from thinking about her. Why had he kept on seeing her? And why had he come on so strong when he knew he would only back her into a corner? She wanted more than sex? Fine. Let her find some nice boring guy who wanted his dinner on the table promptly at six every evening, and live happily ever after with their two-point-five offspring.

Price had no interest in changing his life, and romantic liaisons were not something to be taken seriously. Still, deep down, he knew that Amanda was different. She deserved better, but not from him. She was the kind of woman who should be courted. The moment the thought entered his head he laughed derisively. What a silly idea, so old-fashioned!

But there was an honesty and a freshness about her that had kept him coming back, even though he berated himself for doing so. The women he dated knew the rules: no promises, no commitments, no messy entanglements. Amanda Hamilton didn't – that much was obvious, or appeared to be. But was she as innocent as she appeared? She was twenty-five and Price had serious reservations whether any woman her age could still be that naïve.

What on earth did she think he wanted? The pleasure of her company? Throw in some sex and that would be exactly right. Was she just putting on an act or was she real? Each time he was with her, his desire to find out increased.

She was all the things that Price was definitely not looking for, yet he couldn't deny that she made him feel like no one else had for a very long time. As he saw it, Amanda was nothing short of dangerous. If he had bothered to put a name to it, he would have had to admit that she made him restless. She made him think of things he didn't want to think about. She made him want more than what he had. She made him want her.

In view of all that, he was reluctant to examine his

reasons for buying her house. Did he really want the house or was he looking for a way to tie her to him, at least for a while longer? He doubted that. After all, he had only to recall their last encounter to feel his anger surge. She knew exactly what he had wanted from her, what every man in his right mind wanted. Only he didn't get it. Instead, he got a stately antebellum mansion, badly in need of repair, a dubious investment at best, in the middle of Only-God-knows-where County.

The closing on the sale of the house was set for the last week in August, six weeks away. Amanda, who was determined not to waste any time thinking about Price, concentrated on deciding what pieces of furniture she would keep and what she would have to sell. It was a heart-wrenching process, since much of it had not only belonged to Margaret, but had been in the family for generations. It was as if she was a traitor, selling out her ancestors and her heritage. But she also knew that she would have to start looking for a place to live and, because of their size and scale, many of the antique pieces would not fit into an apartment.

Her attempts to block out all thoughts of Price would probably have succeeded except for a sudden flurry of activity that began one Monday morning. She had barely had her first cup of coffee when she heard the doorbell. Looking out the window, she was surprised to see a white pickup truck parked in the drive. Cautiously, she opened the door. It was her first mistake.

'Good morning, are you Ms Hamilton? Mr McCord sent me out here to give him an estimate to replace the heating and air conditioning system. He said you wouldn't mind letting me take a look at it since he's buying the house from you.'

And so it went on for the rest of the week. A steady stream of people found their way to her door: a plumbing contractor, an electrician, a painting contractor, and a roofing contractor. All of them sent by Price. When Amanda tried to tell them that the fact that Mr McCord had sent them out didn't mean anything because he didn't own the house yet, and that she, of course, was under no obligation to let them in, it didn't seem to matter. In each case, she would finally relent because, as they all reminded her, it was a long drive out there.

Amanda was aggravated by Price's expectations and irritated by all the interruptions, but she wasn't about to put herself in a position where she would have to call him to complain. Besides, she wasn't even sure he would take her call.

It was raining. Heavy clouds had turned the afternoon prematurely dark as Amanda ran the last few metres to the small bar that Joan and her friends often used as a meeting place. It was Friday night and in a matter of minutes the place would be filled with the after-work crowd. The dark wood panelling and stained glass created a cosy atmosphere. It felt good to be out of the rain, but Amanda wished she hadn't agreed to show up.

Joan would want to hear all the arrangements she had made for moving, and where she had looked for apartments. In fact, Amanda hadn't done any of those things — yet. This whole moving process was not going well. It had been further complicated by the number of people Price had sent out to the house ostensibly to measure and to give estimates. In reality, she was beginning to suspect he had done it simply to irritate her.

As soon as they ordered their drinks, Joan began to ask Amanda all the questions she didn't want to answer.

'You know, Amanda, you're just trying to ignore the fact that you're selling your house. You can't ignore that any more than you can ignore who the buyer is.'

'Joan...' groaned Amanda.

'I know you better than anyone,' interrupted Joan, 'and I suspect you're involved with Price.'

'I am not "involved",' argued Amanda. 'I haven't seen him in quite a while, nor am I likely to until the closing. He was only interested in the house, not me.'

'Hmm. Nice try, but it's written all over your face. You're miserable because of him.'

'Sorry, Joan. The only thing I'm miserable about is the steady stream of people Price has sent out to my house for one reason or another.'

'Come on,' Joan said. 'I'm your best friend. What's really going on between the two of you?'

'Nothing.' *Absolutely nothing.*

'Why not? Obviously you're attracted to him.'

Since Amanda was sure that Joan wouldn't discontinue this interrogation until she explained things, she told Joan about her last meeting with Price, leaving out many of the details. But Joan was quick to fill in the blanks. 'So he wants to play adult games and you think you're not ready,' concluded Joan.

Amanda nodded.

'Amanda, maybe this could be the real thing,' said Joan almost wistfully.

'Maybe, but I'll just be another in a long line of affairs for him.'

'Lots of relationships begin in bed.'

'He already suspects that my experience with men is, uh, limited. Who am I kidding? He questioned me and tried to get me to tell him exactly how many sexual relationships I had had. I told him it was none of his business. I certainly couldn't tell him the truth. He probably wouldn't believe that either.'

Joan signalled the waitress for a refill, then focused her attention on Amanda. 'I have never understood your hangups about sex.'

'That's because you don't have any.'

'That's not entirely true,' said Joan. 'I don't sleep with every man who comes along. I am discriminating,' she said in a hurt voice.

'I'm sorry, Joan. That is none of my business, and I didn't mean it the way it sounded. But you have to understand, I'm not like you. I can't handle sex on a casual basis. It's not a casual thing with me.'

'What about you and Brian?' asked Joan. 'You seemed to care a lot for him.'

'That was a long time ago and, yes, I did care for him but he never excited me the way Price does. There was something missing. I wanted more.'

'But not as much as Price has to offer?' Joan asked candidly.

'Honestly, I don't know. Yes. I want the kind of excitement I feel when I'm with him. No one has ever made me feel that way. It's like I'm doing something dangerous by just being near him. But I'm looking for someone to love. I want a man who wants to spend the rest of his life with me. Price is just looking for some short-term entertainment.'

'Take what he offers, Amanda. Experience life instead of wasting time watching it pass you by. For some women, men like Price McCord never come along.'

The conversation kept replaying itself as Amanda drove home along the dark, rain-slicked roads. This was the same conversation that the two friends had had many times before, and Amanda always shrugged off Joan's advice. They were two different people. Where Joan was aggressive and open about sex, Amanda was reticent and afraid to get involved. Until tonight. Maybe Joan was right – maybe it *was* time to take a chance.

chapter four

Amanda hoped there would be no more interruptions this afternoon. Before she tackled the unpleasant process of packing and moving, she wanted to finish the illustrations for a book on sea animals. Some of the watercolours she had done earlier in the week were satisfactory, but her attempts for the past two days were not up to her usual standards. Most of this she attributed to her lack of concentration. Running through her mind were thoughts about the last time she was with Price, and her conversation the other night with Joan. The rest she could chalk up to the number of interruptions she had had.

Two hours later, she had just completed several sketches when she heard a car coming up the drive. She groaned. This time she was not going to be accommodating. She wasn't even going to be nice. She was fed up, and she didn't care how far this person had driven. Throwing her pencil aside, she resolutely marched to the front door. Immediately she recognised the woman as the same one who had been with Price that day at the restaurant. For a moment, Amanda was speechless.

The auburn-haired woman looked to be about the same age as she was, but there the similarity ended. Her bearing and her impeccable clothing spoke of supreme self-confidence. As she skirted Amanda and stepped uninvited into the house, she announced airily and certainly to no one in particular, that she was here to look at Price's new house.

'I'm doing the interior. Oh, oh! Lovely, beautiful, but I see major renovations coming. Lots of work to be done here,' she said looking toward the ceiling, then at the worn but highly polished hardwood floors. Peering into Amanda's studio, she turned slightly toward Amanda and said over her shoulder, 'Are all the walls plaster? Oh, by the way I'm Caroline Sloan. We could definitely use more light in here. Oh, I need to use your phone. My mobile is dead. Where…? Oh, I see it,' she said.

Without waiting for Amanda's permission, Caroline went straight to the desk next to the drawing board and picked up the phone. Suddenly, Amanda was overcome with the urge to do bodily harm to Price and to this obnoxious woman that he had sent out here. Caroline Sloan was probably just masquerading as his interior designer, thought Amanda, angrier than she had been in a long time. She had not forgotten the day she had seen Price and this woman having lunch – the intimate way they spoke to each other, the comfortable body language, the shared laughter. It had been obvious to her, even from her place across the busy restaurant, that the two of them enjoyed more than a business relationship.

Well, this is it. Price McCord has finally pushed me too far! The time has come to show these people exactly who is in charge here!

Without hesitation, Amanda marched toward Caroline, who by now was talking on the phone and scribbling notes, snatched the receiver from Caroline's hand, and slammed it into its cradle.

Caroline's eyes widened.

In a low, steady voice Amanda said, 'Look, whoever you are…'

'Caroline Sloan,' the woman repeated slowly.

'Well, Caroline, make a note of this. You may not use my phone. You are not welcome to look at my house, and you can tell Price McCord not to send another person out here until the sale of this house is completed. It's still my house until the end of August and I'm sick and tired of entertaining his…his *contract labour*!'

Caroline stared at Amanda for a moment, first with surprise and then with amusement as Amanda finished her speech with what was obviously the most insulting description she could muster for all the numerous subcontractors sent by Price, and all the inconvenience they had heaped on her over the past week.

A wide grin broke out on Caroline's face as she said, 'Miss Hamilton…'

'Amanda.'

'Amanda, please don't depend on me to relay your message to Price. A message *that* good deserves to be delivered in person. If I were you, I'd go and see him right now.' Caroline glanced at her watch then added, 'He should be back in his office in about fifteen minutes.' Then she picked up her things, gave Amanda a jaunty salute and departed as swiftly as she had arrived.

For the second time since Caroline had appeared at her door, Amanda was speechless. The woman hadn't appeared to be in the least bit offended by her ranting or her deliberate rudeness.

'I will!' Amanda shouted loudly as Caroline drove away from the house. 'I'll do it right now!'

Quickly, she ran up the stairs to her bedroom and began to search through her wardrobe. It was important that she not only look her best when she confronted Price, she also needed to look like she meant business. Real business, not the kind of monkey business Price had engaged in.

The steel and glass building loomed before Amanda in the late afternoon shadows. Instead of feeling nervous, the sight of the building seemed to calm her. She was here now and she knew exactly what she was going to say and do, having rehearsed it over and over during her drive into the city. She was tired of being taken advantage of, and it was time to let Price know exactly how she felt.

She was through with him, and she was through with

the parade of people he had been sending out to her house. Her plan was to march into his office, say what she had come to say in an emphatic, business-like manner and then exit. With dignity. And authority. And the last word.

The building directory listed 'McCord & Company' on the tenth floor. While Amanda waited for the lift she studied her reflection in the burnished copper door panels. After rummaging through her wardrobe, she had finally decided on a severely tailored grey dress with a white collar and cuffs. Her only jewellery was a pair of silver earrings. As she surveyed her image, Amanda was pleased with the overall effect.

The lift doors opened and she stepped inside, then jabbed the button for the tenth floor. She took comfort in the fact that she at least looked as if she was in control, even though her self-confidence was rapidly deserting her. As the lift whisked her smoothly upward, she felt like she had left her stomach along with her courage on the ground floor. By the time the doors opened, she was nervous and worried that she might have made this trip for nothing.

What if he isn't in?

Caroline Sloan had said he would be here.

Should I have called first?

No, that would only alert him. I want to catch him off guard.

What if he won't see me?

Of course he'll see me. His curiosity would get the best of him. Besides, he could hardly refuse to see a woman he wanted to get in his bed, could he?

Through the glass doors straight ahead she could see the receptionist. Directly over her desk was the McCord name and logo. Just as Amanda approached to announce herself, Price came striding through a set of panelled double doors to the right of the receptionist. Beside him was a woman that Amanda guessed to be in her late fifties.

She was hurriedly making notes on a tablet as Price issued a series of instructions.

The dark blue shirt he wore stretched across his wide shoulders, accentuating his powerful build. He seemed to fill the room with his magnetism. Amanda swallowed as she reached deep inside to gather her courage, reminding herself what had finally spurred her into action. Faintly she attempted to get his attention and when she saw that she had failed she took a deep breath. With much more force she called out to him.

At the sound of her voice, he turned quickly and without missing a beat he acknowledged her presence with a nod and a single word, 'Amanda'. But there was a sudden flare in his dark blue eyes as he took note of her appearance. Then just as suddenly, his gaze became guarded.

But as brief as it had been, Amanda had seen the look in his eyes and it somehow gave her courage. 'Price, I'm hear to talk to you. I have some things I want to say to you.'

'Bad timing, Amanda.' His reply was curt.

'This is important.' Her voice was stronger.

At this, Price raised a questioning eyebrow and looked down at her.

'This is business,' she said firmly.

'I'm on my way out to a job site. You'll have to call me later if you want to talk.'

Amanda could feel her frustration growing. Did he really think he could get rid of her that easily? And, more importantly, was she going to let him just push her aside? What she had to say was damn important and she wanted it said and over with. Now. Quickly she executed a turn, hurried to catch up with him and positioned herself in his path. Price had to break his stride to keep from running over her. He grabbed her by the shoulders to steady both of them.

'All right,' Price said with a slight trace of annoyance,

'but you'll have to come with me while I take care of some things.'

With his hands still on her shoulders, he propelled her around and out of his path, then grabbed her arm to rush her down the hall and back into the lift. Amanda had to double up her steps to keep from being dragged along like so much baggage. Price's secretary rode in the lift with them to the parking garage and she and Price continued to converse in a series of staccato phrases rather than sentences. When they reached the garage, the secretary remained in the lift and pushed the button to return to the tenth floor. Price pulled Amanda along to his car.

'What about my car?' she asked anxiously over her shoulder.

'I'll bring you back here later. You can get it then,' he replied as he opened his car door.

For a moment she wondered if going with him was a wise thing to do, then she shrugged. She hadn't come all this way for nothing.

Turning the key in the ignition, he looked at her as if he were about to say something then, as if he had thought better of the idea, he turned his attention back to the task of driving. Once they had left the parking garage, they rode through streets that were rapidly filling with people on their way home for the evening.

Finally, Amanda took a deep breath and said, 'Price, we have to talk about what you've been doing.'

He didn't respond.

'Are you listening to me?' asked Amanda.

'I've got some serious problems right now, Amanda. That's why I couldn't stop to talk to you. As soon as I take care of a few things we can talk. Then you'll have my full attention and you can tell me about whatever it is you came to see me about.'

It seemed to Amanda that they zigzagged from one side of the city to the other. Each stop was a construction site and the signage identified 'McCord & Company' as the developer and general contractor. Along the way, Price explained what each project was and, in an abbreviated version, outlined the problems he faced at that particular site.

'I had no idea this is what you did,' she said, unable to keep the admiration out of her voice.

'From the time I was a kid, I wanted to build things. I thought being an architect would be enough, but then I discovered that I wanted to be involved with every step of the construction process. So, after three years with a large architectural firm, I started my own company. The first few years were tough. A couple of times I thought I was either going to have to move back in with Mom and Dad, or take a second job just to meet the overhead. My first venture left me in the red. With the second one, I did a little better. It was all a learning process. The turning point was a deal I put together called Cumberland River. By that time, I had wised up and decided that I should be risking somebody else's money, not mine.'

An hour later, when the waning glow of a brilliant pink and orange sunset finally slipped over the horizon and darkness had formed a cosy cocoon around them, Price turned his attention to the woman at his side.

'Now it's just you and me,' he said.

'Well, it's about time,' she replied.

'You know, it's been a while since I've had a woman chase after me like you did today. You managed to provide my staff with quite a scene that will go from pure speculation this afternoon to juicy gossip by coffee break tomorrow morning. It will be interesting to hear just how far they take this afternoon's encounter.'

'Surely not,' Amanda protested. 'You're making it sound like something it's not. Trashy.'

Price grinned suggestively. 'By tomorrow morning it

will be. Especially since we left the building together and your car was still parked in the garage when they all left for the night,' explained Price.

'Well, it's your fault. There's nothing trashy about this,' said Amanda primly. 'This is business.'

'That's too bad. I could do with a little trash from you.'

Amanda sputtered and started to reply, then decided to let it drop. She didn't know whether to take his remark as a compliment or an insult. Sitting up very straight in her seat, she took a deep breath. 'Do I have your full attention?'

'Yes ma'am, you do.'

'Good. Now listen to me. You may have a contract to buy my house, but you don't own it yet. When it's yours you can do whatever you want with it, but until that time I don't want you to send any more people out to my house for any reason. No estimates, no measuring. The one today was the last straw. Your interior designer? Ha! I hardly think so!'

'Caroline? She's harmless. Not always tactful, but a very good designer,' said Price.

'And I'm sure she's good at a lot of other things as well,' Amanda said sarcastically. 'But regardless of her, uh, talents, I mean what I have just said, Price. Not one more person of any variety – and especially not your girl-friend.'

'Caroline isn't my girlfriend.'

'So what is she?'

'My business partner, for one thing.'

'Oh, really? Well, isn't that politically correct.'

Price fought hard to keep his serious expression from turning into a grin. 'You know, Amanda,' he said in a deep and sombre voice, 'this kind of behaviour is not at all what I would expect of you.'

Amanda winced. She wanted to slap him for sounding so pompous. 'I am not fifteen any more, Price, so don't scold me like I am. I hate it when you talk to me in that superior tone of voice as if I'm so much younger and naïve than you are,' Amanda said with fighting spirit.

'Umm...' Price considered his next words to her. 'Maybe it's because you are younger and you don't have a lot of savvy when it comes to male-female relationships. I would hardly describe you as terribly experienced. That much is evident from your behaviour with me the other night.'

'I don't want to talk about that,' she said curtly.

'Well, I do.'

'Listen, Price, just because I wasn't ready to jump at the chance to go to bed with you, doesn't mean anything other than the fact that I'm selective. So don't try to make it into anything else.'

'Selective, hell! Honey, you were ready to bolt and run at the first sign of anything which resembled any kind of intimacy.'

Amanda couldn't acknowledge that he was absolutely right. Her pride wouldn't let her. So she slid down and rested her head against the back of the seat, wishing she had never let herself be goaded into confronting him. Turning her face toward him she said bravely, 'I'm not scared of you, Price McCord. I just don't believe in engaging in intimacy with strangers.'

'By "intimacy with strangers", do you mean having sex with strangers?' Price asked.

Amanda scooted up in her seat, ready for another round of verbal sparring. 'That is precisely what I mean,' she answered, satisfied that she had made her point.

'But you do believe in having sex with men you're well acquainted with,' Price concluded.

Amanda bristled and sat up even straighter. 'I didn't say that. I said I was selective about who I go to bed with.'

'I see, and do I fit your requirements, Amanda? After all, we've known each other for a while. So I'm not exactly a stranger, am I? Or are your standards so high that no ordinary man can possibly meet them? You would be a liar to deny the chemistry between us.'

'Look, Price, I came here to talk to you about business, about the house, certainly not about sex with you or anyone else,' replied Amanda in an effort to extricate herself from a conversation which was causing her to become increasingly uncomfortable. In an effort to change the subject she glanced out the window and realised that nothing around her looked familiar.

'Where are we going?'

'To talk about business. My kind of business,' Price said, his eyes fixed on the street ahead.

'Now wait a minute. You can just take me back to my car. I've said everything I came here to say.'

Price looked away from the street and fixed his dark blue eyes on Amanda. Once more his expression was unreadable. 'But I haven't,' he said quietly.

While Amanda was still struggling to come up with a solution to this situation, he had parked the car and was now holding the door open for her.

'Where are we?' she asked.

He gripped her arm firmly and hurried her from the car toward the steps. 'My apartment,' he answered. A minute later, he unlocked the door with his free hand and pulled her into the foyer.

Amanda stood there not quite knowing what to do. When he released her arm, she reached to push her hair behind her ears. Then, feeling rumpled, she began to pull and tuck at her dress. Nervously, she smoothed non-existent wrinkles.

Price walked by her nonchalantly as if her presence was nothing out of the ordinary. 'You look fine, honey. No need to be nervous.'

'I'm not nervous,' she answered, then raised her chin as if to emphasise her statement.

'Sure you are. But I want you to know that I absolutely will not do anything you don't want me to.'

'Why doesn't that make me feel any better?' Amanda muttered as she glanced around.

The room before her was a monochromatic study in off-whites and near-beiges, quiet colours, accented by stone and glass. The furnishings were contemporary and curiously devoid of personality. Overall, there was nothing she could see that fit the vibrant man she knew Price to be. Venturing further, she walked into the living room. It was meticulous, well ordered, and completely impersonal. Anyone could have lived here.

Hearing Price enter from the kitchen to her right, Amanda indicated the room around her with a sweep of her hand and a touch of bravado. 'Is your partner responsible for decorating this?' Not waiting for his answer she continued, her voice intentionally free of sarcasm but tinged instead with a studied innocence. 'It's really rather...um...cold. Not at all like you. Tell me, did you acquire her services as your personal decorator before she was your, ah, partner or was it the other way around?'

Amanda could sense his displeasure as he purposefully advanced toward her. Sensing his intention, she retreated, staying one step out of his reach until she backed into a wall. Closing in, Price anchored his hands against the hard surface on either side of her. He hadn't touched her, yet she felt trapped by the heat of him.

Shifting his weight, he leaned closer to her. 'Does it matter to you?' he asked in a low controlled voice.

The closer he was, the more difficult it became for her to breathe.

Now he moved even closer, pressing the length of his lean, muscular body against her as his lips took hers in a hard, swift kiss that left her shaken. The power he had over her was breathtaking. She had never known anyone who could make her feel like this.

Amanda swallowed and forced herself to speak, her voice uneven. 'I don't care who you make love to, just as long as it isn't me.'

'Look at me, Amanda,' Price commanded. 'Look at me and tell me that again. And, dammit, for once in your life be honest about what you're feeling – and what you want.'

Slowly Amanda raised her face. Her wide brown eyes locked with his probing dark blue gaze. Unconsciously, she ran the tip of her tongue over her lips. Her answer was cut short by an intense, searing kiss.

His tongue probed her warm mouth and once again he aroused a heat that slowly spread deep within her. He excited and frightened her at the same time. Suddenly, she knew she wanted more, but how could that be, when at the same time she wanted to run away from him? – as far and as fast as she could.

Slowly Price released her lips, but his body still pinned hers. Only by his ragged intake of breath did she suspect that he was also shaken by the force of what had passed between them.

With his head thrown back, he looked down at her and issued his challenge. 'Tell me you don't want me to make love to you, Amanda. Tell me you're afraid to find out what I'll do next. Tell me, and I'll stop.'

A rushing, liquid heat was coursing its way through her body leaving her weak and pliable. She wanted to deny everything that was happening between them. She wanted to tell him to leave her alone. She didn't care if he found out the truth – that she was a woman who was afraid of her own sexuality. Her desperate desire for him was not something she wanted to confront. But suddenly she knew she was no longer in control of her destiny. Her willpower had turned traitor in the face of this incredible encounter. Her lips refused to form the words that would have stopped him. Things had already gone too far. And now she wanted it all.

As he began to unfasten her dress, nothing seemed to matter anymore. She was swept up in a wave of desire, and suddenly it all felt so right. For the first time in her life, Amanda felt beautiful and desirable.

Price read her answer in her eyes. Without words, he picked her up and carried her to his bedroom. He sensed her shyness as he continued the ritual of undressing her, and her vulnerability as first his eyes then his lips claimed her breasts. When his lips moved to cover every inch of her, his husky voice caressed her and encouraged her. When he covered her body with his, she reached for him, wanting more, and wanting to share the pleasure. With his practised touch, he deliberately aroused her, coaxing her to respond to her newly discovered passion.

When his own passion flamed nearly out of control, he throbbed with need. But in spite of the depth and nearly overwhelming desire that he had for Amanda, he had to hear her say she wanted this as much as he did. 'Tell me, babe, now. If you want me to stop...I...will. But if you want to go on, I need to hear you say it. I have to know that you want me as much as I want you.'

Amanda reached for him, her eyes full of wonder. Then she whispered, 'I want you. No one has ever made me feel this way.'

Price took a deep, ragged breath. He was usually a practised, controlled lover, but as the heat between them built, he knew he couldn't wait any longer. He hesitated only a moment before he entered her.

She cried out at his invasion.

Less than a heartbeat later, it was as if a bomb had exploded in his head. He had discovered what Amanda had neglected to tell him. But he couldn't stop now. It was too late.

Price cursed.

Later, Amanda lay next to him on the bed, but he had deliberately turned away from her. With his eyes closed he listened to the sound of his own breathing, rapid and uneven, while he struggled to control the anger he felt towards her for not telling him. Inwardly he cursed his own failure to remain detached from her. He should have never let himself become so emotionally involved. Sex was supposed to be just that, nothing more. The completely unexpected, overpowering passion which had burned and consumed him tonight, was a fire that had raged out of his control.

He felt her touch him softly, then draw her hand away when he didn't respond with an answering caress. He wanted no further intimacy with her, but he knew she wanted to be held by him. And when he couldn't, he felt rotten. He turned towards her then, and saw the confusion in her eyes. But instead of reaching out and taking her in his arms, he settled on his back, covering his eyes with his forearm.

'Price?' Her voice trembled as she brought her hand to his face.

He was consumed by cold, unflinching anger. He was angry at himself for being vulnerable. He didn't want to care this much. Since he and Shelley had gone their separate ways, he had managed to avoid any kind of involvement – at all cost.

When he answered her, his voice was deadly quiet and icy. 'Why didn't you tell me Amanda? What the hell were you thinking of?'

'Would it have made any difference to you, Price?' she answered quietly, fighting to keep her hurt hidden. 'Would it have kept you from making love to me?'

Price took Amanda's small hand from where it rested against his face and set it away from him. 'Yes, it would have made a difference. I might have been hot for you, but I damn well wouldn't have taken you to bed. As a matter of fact, I would have put as much distance between us as possible.'

He paused and drew a deep breath. 'You were right, Amanda, I wanted sex, a fling, a quick lay, all non-committal things. Women like you expect things I'm not prepared to give. You're the kind who puts everything into this one physical act and you want it to last forever. I don't want that kind of intensity – I'm not looking for that and I never wanted you to think I was.'

His breathing was heavy and the room still. 'I don't want any encumbrances, emotional or otherwise. I told you that in the beginning.'

Price was silent again and the minutes seemed to drag on. In a voice that was low and controlled he continued. 'We haven't talked about you. Were you prepared for this?' He hoped to God she was, because he certainly had not taken the precautions he normally would have.

Amanda eyes widened, then the blood rushed to her face as she realised he was talking about birth control. 'Yes,' she stammered, hoping he wouldn't realise she was lying.

'You want this to be about more than sex, don't you?' Price said.

She wanted to put her hands over her ears to shut out the sound of his cold, cutting voice.

'You weren't kidding when you said you were selective, were you? And just think, I was the lucky guy. I just made love to a *virgin*, for heaven's sake, and now I have to deal with your expectations. Tell me something, Amanda, just what is it you think you get from me now?'

chapter five

Price knew he should stop. He was deliberately being cruel, hurting her in a way she didn't deserve, but Amanda was a new kind of danger to him. He was angry at her for not telling him, but he was more disturbed by the intensity of his feelings for her. He hated what he was doing, but a clean break wouldn't leave any doubts as to how things were. There was no room for someone like her in his life.

He heard her move quietly from his side, yet he remained exactly as he was. He knew she had wanted him to reach out and hold her, but he also knew if he did, he would be lost forever.

Amanda gathered her clothes and took them into the adjoining bathroom. She dressed quickly and fought to keep from sobbing. She was hurt and, to the very depths of her soul, she ached with pain like she had never known. Now the thought of having to face Price again caused her to panic. She had to get out of there.

Fully dressed, she opened the bathroom door then quietly closed it behind her. She could hear Price in the kitchen, and she was relieved that she wouldn't have to face him again. She couldn't.

Grabbing her bag off the table in the foyer, she hurried out of the front door. Blindly, she began to run. It was dark and she was glad that no one could see the tears she had held for so long as they began an unending trail down her cheeks. Finally, she slowed to a walk. She had no concept of time and it was impossible to say how long she had been walking. It didn't matter.

Her first impulse when she reached the all-night

convenience store was to call Joan to come and get her, but she knew she couldn't face that kind of humiliation – even with her best friend. Joan would want to know what had happened. She would never have understood how she felt. Joan had been in and out of too many love affairs to understand how devastated she was. Instead, Amanda called a taxi to take her to her car.

It wasn't her fault she had been a virgin all this time! She would have changed that a long time ago if she could have just found the right man, but she hadn't. Then for a long time it didn't seem important. Until tonight. She had finally found the right man, and she had given not only herself to him, she had also given him her heart. And he had betrayed her in the worst possible way – he had made love to her and then rejected her. And broken her heart in the process.

Later that night, when she tried to reconstruct things, she could not remember getting her car from the parking lot or even driving home. In spite of the fact that it was a typically warm night, she was chilled. When she remembered how she had unconditionally made love to Price, she began to shiver. Early in her adult life she realised that men like Price didn't marry women like her. They didn't marry anyone. They didn't have to. There were always hoards of beautiful women available. She hadn't planned this – it had just happened. To have Price so coldly and cuttingly make the accusations he had, hurt her deeply.

He had used her. No, he hadn't used her. He had given her a choice, but afterwards he had made it very clear that sex was all he was interested in. Amanda sobbed into her pillow. She didn't deserve the treatment he had given her.

The next morning she couldn't get out of bed. She alternated between crying and sleeping fitfully. By the second day, she couldn't remember when she had last eaten. The phone went unanswered. When she awoke the third day, the hurt had been replaced by a cold numbness and a hard resolve. She could go on with her life. Each day would be a little easier.

Amanda threw herself into her work with such fervour that she no longer spent her days and nights thinking about Price. She had contacted the publishers she had previously worked with, and took on as much work as they could give her. Some assignments had almost impossible deadlines. More often than not, she worked into the early hours of the morning until she could no longer see. Then she fell into bed exhausted. Her work became the focus of her existence.

Days turned into weeks and she lost track of everything except the deadlines she had to meet. She avoided anything having to do with moving, because she would once again be reminded of Price and the intense hurt he had caused. It had been almost a month since that terrible night in June. The closing on the house was set for the last week in August. Until then, she didn't have to think about him.

The interlude with Price was a personal and private thing to Amanda, and for that reason she had never spoken of it to Joan. During the times they had talked, Joan had sensed a change. To her, Amanda seemed even more serious than usual and she was spending all her time working. Joan made several attempts to get Amanda to go to parties with her, but Amanda always used work as her excuse for declining these invitations.

Even though Joan suspected the change in Amanda had something to do with Price McCord, she was positive that Amanda had not taken Price up on his offer. While she might secretly wish that she had, anyone who knew Amanda Hamilton would tell you that, without a doubt, she had not gone to bed with him.

Joan was, of course, one hundred per cent wrong!

Caroline, who was perched on the corner of a low filing cabinet in Price's office, was waiting for an answer. 'Should I repeat the question?' she asked after a long silence. For days now, Price had been irritable and she wanted to know why.

Price straightened his shoulders and ran his hands over his face. Scattered across the drafting table in front of him were the plans for 'McCord & Company's newest development. Now that he had finally located the right piece of property, he had thrown himself into this project as if he were driven, working late into the night and coming in early most mornings. Laying his pencil down, Price slowly swivelled on his stool then propped his elbows on the table behind him, letting his hands dangle. He stretched his long legs out, crossing them at the ankles as if he were completely relaxed. But his careless pose belied the piercing gaze he fixed on the woman before him.

'No, Sweet Caroline,' he said, using her childhood name. 'I heard the question and the answer is none of your business. Now get out of here, and go find somewhere else to decorate with your presence besides my office.'

'Well,' Caroline said, 'aren't we snotty today! What's eating at you, Price? Working with you used to be fun, but now you're grouchy all the time. Your attitude is rubbing off on everyone around you.'

'Certainly not on you, Caroline. You were born snotty and you've always had a bad attitude.'

'Then I guess maybe we share some of the same family traits after all,' she replied. Then her voice softened as she continued. 'It's a wonder anyone can stand to be around you, big brother.'

'Does that mean you're leaving now?' Price slowly eased himself out of his chair, ambled over to Caroline and planted an affectionate kiss on her forehead and said, 'You're a better business partner than you are a sister.

Partners don't pry into each other's personal lives. Unfortunately, sisters seem to think they have that right. Now get out of here so I can get back to work.'

Caroline McCord Sloan uncrossed her long legs, slid off the cabinet and smiled at Price as she left the workroom. She loved her older brother dearly. He was the one person besides her husband who would always be supportive of her. But she was concerned. She had never seen Price act so moody and withdrawn. All week long he had snapped at people at the slightest provocation. She couldn't seem to pinpoint the cause, nor had she been able to get Price to tell her what was bothering him. But she was nothing if not tenacious. Sooner or later, she would figure this out.

Above all, she wanted Price to be as happy as she was. He needed someone to love, and someone who would love him back. She thought he had found that with Shelley, but that was before they had split up. Briefly the image of Amanda Hamilton floated across her mind. She lacked Shelley's dramatic looks, but she was pretty in a delicate sort of way. But Price would never be interested in someone like her – or would he? There had been plenty of sparks coming from Amanda the afternoon Caroline had gone out to her house. Did Amanda's impulsive visit to their office last week have anything to do with Price's present state of mind?

Caroline looked back over her shoulder at her brother who was once more bent over the drafting table. Then she closed the office door behind her. Price and Amanda. It was an interesting premise, certainly an unlikely paring, but it was enough to spur her imagination. Caroline decided to do some detective work. The right to pry into her brother's personal life was one of the great benefits of being his little sister!

'This time I won't take no for an answer,' said Joan.

Amanda, who was not feeling the least bit sociable, wished her friend would just leave her alone. Even though she voiced that thought several times, Joan ignored her, acting like she hadn't heard. So Amanda held the phone away from her ear with one hand while she continued to draw with the other. Now that she was feeling more in control of her emotions, she didn't want to disrupt her work routine.

'Are you listening to me, Amanda? Your birthday is next week and I'm getting some friends together to celebrate. Just a group. No dates, I promise. And this time I won't let you use work as an excuse to beg off. No one should work on their birthday, so be ready to go out.'

Amanda groaned. She didn't even want to think about her birthday. It was an unpleasant reminder that another year had passed, and her future, which hadn't been all that bright to begin with, was looking increasingly dismal.

'It'll be fun, and you've been such a drudge lately that you need a break,' said Joan. 'I'll call you later in the week with all the details. But I will tell you that we're going someplace fancy, so plan to buy yourself a knockout dress. You never know who you might meet.'

Replacing the receiver, Amanda sighed in defeat and admitted it might be good to get out. *OK*, she thought, *I'll do it – new dress and all*. Shopping would give her something to do besides working, sleeping, and trying not to think about that night with Price.

The reflection in the full-length mirror confirmed that she had lost weight in the past few weeks. The new dress she had bought for her birthday was laid out on the bed, a black silk crepe that skimmed her body like a slip and provided just the kind of look she wanted. She turned, looking over her shoulder to get a view of the back, and she was glad she had decided to try something different. The old Amanda would have selected something that resembled a prom dress, or worse, a bridesmaid dress. This Amanda, she decided, looked elegant and seductive.

Her shiny brown hair was pulled back and twisted up. With strands hanging loose, the effect was sophisticated. Diamante earrings that glittered above her bare shoulders were her only adornment. Reaching for her beaded evening bag, Amanda studied her reflection once more. On the occasion of her twenty-sixth birthday, she felt beautiful.

When she arrived at the club, she had been surprised and pleased at the number of friends that were there. Just being out with people again was refreshing. The evening was definitely going to be a success.

The club Joan had selected was new, but was already one of the trendiest places in Atlanta. Joan had been there before but Amanda never had. Joining the friends Joan had assembled, she felt suddenly carefree. It was nice to feel this way again, she thought, especially after the past few weeks. Now, as she recalled her conversation with Joan, Amanda was glad that her friend had been persistent.

When the band began to play, Steve Quinn asked her to dance. For most of the evening he had been especially attentive and, even though she suspected that he might be doing so only because Joan had asked him to, she was still flattered.

On the other side of the club, Caroline Sloan watched the couples on the dance floor as they moved to the rhythm of the music. Her attention was caught by one couple in particular. The woman looked familiar. After a few minutes she turned away from her husband, Mike, and motioned to her brother to lean closer. 'Look, Price,' said Caroline, 'the woman in the black dress dancing with the tall blond man, isn't that Amanda Hamilton?'

Price didn't reply immediately. Instead, he leaned to his

left to get a better look at the dance floor. Then his eyes darkened.

'Yes, I believe it is,' he answered smoothly, careful to hide the sudden tension that gripped him.

'Another old friend, Price? You must know every single woman in Atlanta,' his companion said teasingly. Sara Armstrong was Caroline's friend and house guest.

'A business acquaintance,' replied Price, turning his attention to Sara.

'Price is buying her house,' said Caroline, leaning forward. 'It's a wonderful old place, but it is going to need a lot of work. I can't wait to get started on it. Not much has been done to it in all these years. The interior will be a real challenge. Of course, I...'

'Caroline,' Price said, 'let's wait a while, until I decide what to do with the house. I think I want to settle into it and get a feel for it before I consider any changes. I may leave it just the way it is.'

Caroline frowned. 'You're not serious?'

'Yes, I am,' answered Price, then he turned to the woman next to him. 'Will you excuse me for a few minutes, Sara? I have something I need to discuss with Miss Hamilton.'

'I have to leave soon, Price, so don't hurry back on my part.' Sara glanced at her watch. 'My flight home leaves at six in the morning so I have to get up early. Caroline, you and Mike stay. I can catch a taxi.'

'Absolutely not,' said Caroline. 'Besides, I suspect Mike is ready to go too.'

Price leaned down, kissed his sister, then Sara, and shook his brother-in-law's hand.

'It was good to see you again,' Sara said.

As they finished their drinks, Caroline turned and watched her brother cross the room purposefully. From his stride, she could tell that this was not going to be a business discussion. She couldn't shake off the feeling that Amanda Hamilton was definitely at the root of Price's recent moodiness. This, she was sure, was an encounter that would bear watching.

The band had started to play again, this time an old love song, one that seemed to transcend time and generations. The melody was haunting, the words painful and sad. Amanda was still standing beside the table along with several others when Price approached, touched her arm, then turned her towards him.

Her heart nearly stopped at the sight of him. For a moment she felt the same intense pain she had experienced when she had last seen him, and the equally intense yearning. Without a word to her or the party she was with, Price tugged at her arm, motioning for her to come with him then proceeded to lead her toward the exit.

Coming to her senses, Amanda tried to pull her arm from his grasp. Finding her voice she said, 'Let me go! What do you think you're doing?'

'We're going outside for a private conversation.'

'No, we're not,' she replied as once again she tried to shake his grasp. 'I'm here with friends and I'm not going anywhere with you.'

Price looked down at her and released his hold on her arm. 'Your call,' he said and he reached for her hand to lead her back through the crowd on to the dance floor, where he turned and pulled her into his arms.

She was much closer than she wanted to be and intensely aware of his body, the same hard, muscular body that had so completely taken possession of hers. Fighting for space between them, Amanda was struggling at the same time to bring her racing heart under control. 'Please, let me go, Price.'

He relaxed his hold allowing some space between them. Tilting his head back, he ran his eyes assessingly over her. 'You look different tonight. Quite a change,' he said as he continued to observe her from beneath hooded eyes.

'Of course I've changed,' she answered sharply. 'What did you expect? Tonight I look like the kind of woman you usually take home to bed.'

Price didn't comment. Instead he drew Amanda closer as the music lulled them into a greater awareness of each other.

This man is dangerous, she thought, feeling the tension building between them. *He has a magnetism that I can't seem to resist.* Nestled against him, she had nearly let herself be lulled into a state of lethargy. The soft, sensual music and darkness combined with the smell of him, the nearness of him. She wanted nothing more than for this to go on forever, yet she knew she could not make the same mistake twice.

Price leaned down, his lips touching first her hair then the soft skin at her temple. 'I've missed you, babe.'

She wanted to tell him that he couldn't have missed her too much since he hadn't tried to call or see her since that night. And no matter how much she wanted to believe him, one quick look across the room told her she would be a fool to do so. He certainly wasn't lacking for female companionship. She had recognised Caroline Sloan immediately, but she didn't know the other couple.

Instead of answering him, Amanda gave him a wry smile. It said so much more than words could have.

'Can you get away from your friends later?' he asked in a husky voice, ignoring her unspoken message.

She shook her head. 'I can't,' she whispered. Amanda wanted to be strong about this, but she could feel the magic of him threatening to wipe out all her resistance.

Price pulled her even closer as their bodies swayed together to the music. 'Meet me later, Amanda. I've got to see you.'

'What about your date?'

Price looked over toward the table where he had been sitting. It was empty. 'They had to leave. Meet me out front in a half-hour. We'll go somewhere quiet for a drink. We can talk.' His lips touched close to Amanda's ear, and she could feel the warmth of his breath. 'I need to see you. Don't disappoint me.'

Without meaning to, she let her fingers wander up to the soft hair at the nape of his neck. The feel and smell of him was intoxicating.

'I don't have my car here,' Price said softly as he pulled away to look at her.

'We can take my car,' she whispered breathlessly, then realised that she had just surrendered.

When she was once again seated at the table with her friends, Joan was full of questions. Amanda glared at her but Joan, oblivious to Amanda's silent warning, continued to pry.

Charlie O'Donnell, a scholarly looking man with glasses whom Amanda had never met before tonight, leaned over and put his arm around Joan. 'Give Amanda a break, honey. If she wants you to know something, she can tell you later when there are not so many people around.'

Joan turned at the sound of his voice. 'You're right, Charlie.'

Earlier that evening, Amanda wondered if he and Joan were dating, then she immediately dismissed the idea. He was definitely not the type of man Joan went after. But just now, when she looked at Joan, she realised that Charlie was the guy – the same one Joan had told her about.

Thirty minutes later, Amanda made her excuses and thanked everyone for a wonderful birthday. When she walked outside, the night air seemed to clear her head and help her put things in perspective. Price was still inside, but she knew he would soon be waiting for her at the entrance to the club where they had agreed to meet. Charlie and Steve had frowned at the idea of her walking to her car by herself and both men had offered to go with her, but she had declined. She needed a few minutes alone.

Now that she was no longer captive in Price's arms, the thought of what she was about to do took on an entirely new perspective. How could she even contemplate going anywhere with him after what he had done to her? How could she stand the hurt and humiliation once more of wanting him and knowing he didn't feel the same way about her? He had made it clear that he didn't want to be encumbered with any expectations that she, as a recently deflowered virgin, might have.

Amanda walked quickly to her car and got in, wishing she had never agreed to meet him. Looking toward the entrance to the club, she located Price. She started the car and backed out of the parking space. Did she want him? In the worst way. She wanted him to make love to her from the top of her head to the tips of her toes – but she wanted to be more to him than what she was.

Approaching the entrance, Amanda slowed the car and for a brief instant she regretted what she was about to do. But she could not go anywhere with Price McCord. Not tonight, not ever.

Price stepped off the curb as her car came nearly to a stop, He smiled, took another step forward, then leaned down to peer through the glass of the car's window. As he reached for the door handle, his eyes met Amanda's for a moment. But the answering smile he anticipated wasn't there. Instead, a look that resembled regret crossed Amanda's face. Suddenly, and without warning, she slammed her foot down on the accelerator. With a squeal she sped off, leaving him standing in the street, a stunned expression on his handsome face.

The contents of the decanter were far less than what they had been two hours ago, yet the effects had not been proportionate to the amount of liquor Price had consumed.

His long length was stretched out on the sofa while his feet rested on the coffee table. With his head thrown back, he studied the contents of his glass intently as if it held the answer to all his problems.

He had been astounded when she had driven off without him. Chalk one up for Amanda... she was the first one ever to run. He was accustomed to women who went to great lengths to make themselves available to him. He hadn't worried about rejection since he was thirteen, when his mother began complaining about the number of girls who called at the house for him.

In the hours since he had hailed a taxi to take him home from the club, Price had gone through several phases, the strongest having been anger at Amanda for humiliating him like that. Then there was the anger he directed at himself, for believing she couldn't possibly turn him down.

In spite of every rotten thing he had said to her the night they had made love, about her failure to warn him she was still a virgin, about what she would expect from him, he still wanted her. Thinking back to that night, the awful way he had treated her, it was no wonder she had run from him.

Amanda excited him as no other woman had. She enchanted him and aroused in him an incredible passion, one he had only experienced with her. Unwillingly, he also admitted to a curious desire to protect her from anyone who might hurt her. How much sense did that make now, when he had probably hurt her like no one else ever had?

Now some hours and quite a few drinks later, Price acknowledged the irony of the situation. Absurdly, he had ignored Amanda until tonight when they had met quite by accident. Even without taking into consideration their previous night together, he had been so egotistical, and so intent upon satisfying his craving for her, as to expect her to readily agree to spend another night with him.

'She could have at least had the decency to say no,' he muttered, but then he realised that he would have promised whatever it took to change her mind. Price downed the rest of his drink. What a picture he must have made. Long considered one of the city's most eligible bachelors, he had been left standing in the gutter with only the exhaust fumes from her car to keep him company.

Curiously, Amanda felt that tonight had helped her put her feelings in order. She still wanted Price desperately, but now she was in control. Some might have viewed what she did as amusing, or even harsh, but for her it was an act of pure courage. She would not settle for less than what she really wanted.

Only she knew how close she had come to going with him tonight, and that had made her feel weak and ashamed. It had taken all her combined strength and pride to leave him behind, to run from him. The thought of reliving the pain he had caused her to feel after their first night together had only served to strengthen her resolve. She couldn't go through that again.

The sun was shining brightly the next morning. Amanda had always believed that daylight was largely responsible for keeping events of the world in perspective. Nothing ever looked as bad when examined in the bright light of the sun, as it did in the deceptive glow of the moon.

Leaning back in her chair, she replaced her pencil in the coffee cup that held an assortment of artist's tools. She stretched her hands high in the air before folding them on the top of her head and was glad that this was her last assignment with a tight deadline. Once the illustrations for this book were completed, she planned to resume a more sensible schedule.

Amanda's gaze wandered over to the long floor-length windows and beyond to the stately trees that surrounded the old house she so dearly loved. With all her heart, she wished she could have found a way keep this place, but it was impossible. The idea of selling it to Price was disturbing, especially since she had been so stupid as to make love with him. It troubled her that she had no other choice. She had accepted his offer, the contract had been signed, and she knew it was the best deal she was going to get.

Joan had called earlier wanting to know the outcome of the previous night. Instead of supplying details, Amanda thanked her sincerely for a wonderful birthday celebration. Joan countered with more questions about Price.

At each turn, Amanda skilfully turned the conversation away from Price until finally, unable to stand it any longer, Joan said, 'Enough of these evasive answers, Amanda. Are you going to tell me about you and Price or not?'

'No, I'm not,' answered Amanda, 'because there's nothing to tell.'

'Nothing to tell?' wailed Joan incredulously. 'The man was practically making love to you on the dance floor. I've never seen anything so sensuous in all my life – not in public anyway.'

'That's ridiculous, Joan. He hardly even touched me.'

'It was all in the eyes and the body language.'

'You've been reading too many books, or watching too many movies, Joan. Now tell me about your trip next week.'

Amanda had been relieved that she had been able to steer the conversation to other things. But now as she remembered yesterday evening, she wondered if their attraction for each other had really been that obvious. Closing her eyes she recalled how it had felt to be held close in his arms, the heat that had seemed to spread through her veins when he touched her. How everything around her seemed to fade away, leaving her only aware of him.

Maybe Joan was right. Hmmm... Amanda Hamilton engaging in a shameful public display of affection and, surprisingly, she wasn't the least embarrassed by it. She had definitely changed, all right. She was a new woman – a sensuous, seductive woman, who looked and felt sinful in black silk – a woman in charge of her destiny.

The realisation brought a satisfied smile to her lips.

chapter six

The office was quiet. Price's secretary had come in earlier to see if he needed anything else before she left for the evening. It seemed that these days it took him longer to get things done. Thoughts of Amanda frequently caused him to lose his concentration. She had surprised him the other night. He was so accustomed to women who were agreeable to whatever he suggested that he had been shocked at her actions. He still hadn't got over it.

He stood and stretched, once again wondering what he was going to do about her. He wanted her. He hadn't been out with anyone else since the night they had made love. Even though the urge to pick up the phone and call her was strong, he resisted. For as powerful as his desire was, he didn't want the encumbrance that having her would mean, and the guilt he would feel afterward. But he was finding it difficult to dismiss her. She was more than a challenge. He could handle challenges – he thrived on them. But Amanda, she scared the hell out of him.

Amanda walked through the house mentally taking inventory. There were boxes in each room, neatly stacked and labelled with the contents. It didn't seem possible, but the closing on the sale of the house was only a few days away. She would soon be moving to a new place. With Joan's help, she had finally found an apartment and had put a deposit on it, but she had agonised during the entire process.

The apartment was in a good section of Atlanta that had once been fashionable, then terribly run down, and was now in vogue again. The entire area had undergone renovation and was mostly populated by singles and young couples. Because it was an older building, the apartment had some architecturally interesting features that appealed to Amanda's creative eye. It was going to be OK, she decided.

Looking around, she was sad to think of leaving her house. The furniture she couldn't use was going into storage. She couldn't bring herself to sell the things that had meant so much to her grandmother. Maybe she would later, after she had adjusted to her new place and to her new life. At one point, she had considered asking Price to keep some of her things here until she made up her mind what to do with them. But that was before she had decided to stay as far away from him as possible. Of course, she really didn't have to worry about that. He hadn't attempted to get in touch with her since her birthday.

'So much for romance, sweet memories and all that nonsense,' Amanda muttered aloud, recalling Joan's advice to embrace life by taking some risks. It was painfully obvious that Price was only interested in a repeat performance of their one-night-stand and when he didn't get what he wanted, he had moved on to better hunting grounds.

Amanda sat down in the middle of the floor. Wiping her forehead with the sleeve of her shirt, she looked around knowing how much she would miss living here. How could she not, when this enchanting old house held so many memories of her youth? For years it had provided so much more than shelter. It was her security, the place where she would always be loved and wanted, the place where she could hide when the outside world became too harsh.

Later that night, she wandered through the house, taking in all the beautiful details and all the imperfections she had come to love, memorising them by sight and touch, imagining what it would be like not to live here anymore. How would it feel to know that Price McCord occupied her home – this beautiful, tranquil place where she had found such peace and love and security.

For more than ten years it had been her refuge – since the summer after her father died. She had turned fifteen that year and her mother, Susan, had left her there with Margaret, her father's mother. Just for a visit, Susan had assured the anxious child. But then winter came and Amanda, who had been anticipating the return home and the coming year at her old school, waited in vain for her mother to come for her. Instead, she had remained with Margaret. Then, when it was time, Margaret had enrolled Amanda in school.

In all the summers that followed, there had been occasional visits from her mother, but Amanda, given no other choice, lived with her grandmother. In time, she realised that Margaret Hamilton was the only person in her life she could count on.

Then six months ago, Susan had returned once more, this time for Margaret's funeral, but she departed soon afterward, offering no support – emotional or financial – to her only child. The bond that should have existed between mother and daughter had disintegrated long ago, leaving the two women nothing more than polite strangers.

Left alone to straighten out Margaret's affairs, and faced with the prospect of losing the house, Amanda soon realised that she was fighting a battle she couldn't win. First she had lost her father, then her mother, then her grandmother. Now it was nearly over. The house and the fifty acres of land that went with it had been sold. It seemed to Amanda that she was destined to lose everything she loved.

Still, she believed she was doing the right thing. It was

time she stopped hiding and started to build a life. It was time to think about herself and her future. Judging by what had happened so far, it certainly didn't look as if there was going to be a man around to take care of her.

Sam Johnson cleared his throat, mostly to break the silence in the small conference room. A few minutes later, George Hudson, the attorney who was handling this closing did the same. Sam wished that things were not as strained as they appeared to be between Price and Amanda. Most of all, he hoped that the closing would proceed smoothly.

Price was seated on one side of the table looking stern in his dark suit. The pristine whiteness of his shirt only served to accentuate his tan and his startling blue eyes. His relaxed pose contradicted the intensity with which he watched Amanda.

On the other side of the walnut conference table, Amanda sat with her hands clenched in her lap. She had dressed with care, knowing that she would be subject to Price's scrutiny. Her navy trouser suit was softened by the addition of a gold necklace and earrings. Amanda did not want to encourage any discussion with Price that did not have anything to do directly with the actual transfer of property. She especially wanted him to avoid any mention of their last meeting in front of Sam.

Her eyes met Price's over the conference table, but there was no warmth there. She could have been someone he was meeting for the first time. When she had arrived, he had stood, his greeting polite but distant. From that moment on, he had not bothered to initiate any conversation except with Sam or George.

Sam excused himself and left them while he went into his office for some papers he had forgotten. 'Stubborn,' he muttered. 'Hostile,' he said as he riffled through the stack of file folders on his desk. Finding the papers he was looking for, he headed back down the hall to the conference room. 'Couple of damn fools. Anyone can see they're perfect for each other.'

In the conference room, Amanda adjusted her jacket then looked around the room. She smiled at the attorney, and responded when he made a comment about the weather. But she refused to let her eyes meet Price's. *Say something, please, anything.*

But Price continued to watch her in silence.

All right, if you won't speak, I will.

'How have you been, Price?'

'Fine, and you?'

'As good as I can be under the circumstances. I hope you'll take good care of the place and grow to love it as much as I do.' Amanda's voice wavered with emotion, but only for a moment.

'I'll take care of it,' he said quietly.

Price turned toward Sam when he returned, and Amanda took advantage of the opportunity to study his profile. Had she really expected him to treat her differently?

No, not under the circumstances.

Yes, she had. Dammit! She wasn't a stranger to him — they had been intimate. She blushed at the thought while she continued to stare at him.

'Do you see something that interests you, Amanda?' he asked lazily.

Knowing perfectly well that his question was a direct reference to their night together, she answered with a wistful smile. 'No, I only thought I did.'

Ouch. Price decided he would be better off if he kept his mind on the business at hand instead of Amanda. Idly he wondered what he was doing here, buying a house he neither wanted nor needed. No, that wasn't entirely true. He did want the house, and a few nights ago he had finally admitted that he wanted Amanda — even on her terms.

When he dissected his reasons, he admitted in all fairness that he had done everything he could think of to distance himself from her. He had thought that his harsh treatment of her would be the end of their association, but he hadn't counted on his desire for her. Neither had he counted on Amanda being such a worthy adversary.

During the next hour, Price and Amanda went through the process of transferring real property from seller to buyer. Since this was a first for Amanda, she had to ask George to explain things to her as they went along. Several times she wanted to put a stop to things. She didn't want to go through with the sale, but she knew she had no alternative.

As they each signed the final set of papers, Sam, along with George Hudson, breathed a sigh of relief. Sam wouldn't have been the least bit surprised if one or the other had called a halt before the transaction was complete. Now it was done. Once again, he thought about Margaret's house passing out of the family after so many generations. Then he thought about the effort Amanda had expended to try to keep the house, and he knew she had done the right thing. He only hoped that her life from here on would be a lot more carefree than it had been.

When it was over, they all stood. Sam shook hands with Price and gave Amanda a hug. 'This is the right thing, you know.'

'Thank you, Sam,' she said. 'I would never have made it through this if it hadn't been for you. I know I'll feel better in a few days, once I get settled.' She would be moving the day after tomorrow.

In a surprise manoeuvre, Price took Amanda's arm as they exited the building together. For a split second she considered yanking it away, but Sam and George were close behind them and she didn't want to make a scene. This had not been an easy day for Sam either.

'We'll take my car,' he said. 'Yours brings back unpleasant memories.'

Amanda knew this was a reference to the night of her birthday when she had driven off and left him standing in front of the club. 'Wait a minute, I'm...'

He held up a hand to forestall any further objections. 'We're going to dinner. You owe me that much after what you did to me.'

'I don't owe you anything,' Amanda snapped, 'and I'm certainly not going to dinner with you.'

'Aw, come on, Amanda. Let's declare a truce. Just for tonight. It isn't every day that you sell a house or I buy one. Whatever our reasons, it's a time to celebrate.'

'For you maybe. You have...my home.'

'For you too. It can be a farewell,' Price said gently, knowing that this was an emotional time for her.

Amanda sighed. Maybe if she just faced this event head-on, she would get past the sadness. If she went back to the house right now, she would just spend the night feeling sorry for herself.

'OK,' she said. 'But you have to bring me back right after dinner.'

Secretly, Price breathed a sigh of relief. He hadn't been sure he could convince Amanda to go with him.

It was almost seven in the evening and daylight had faded to a softer, diffused shade of pink. Their destination was a small restaurant, known for its superb food and atmosphere. It was quiet, charming and relaxed. Both of them avoided topics that were too personal and, after a while, Amanda began to relax and enjoy herself.

It was Price who steered the conversation back to the house he had just bought. 'You must have mixed feelings about selling the house to me.'

'The decision to sell was difficult, no matter who the buyer.'

'But more difficult to see me buy it?' asked Price.

Amanda looked into his eyes. 'Yes,' she said simply.

'I'll take good care of it, Amanda,' he promised. 'I plan to live there for a while before I begin any repairs.'

'And how convenient that you already have all your estimates for the repairs,' she pointed out with undisguised sarcasm.

Under his white collar, Price flushed.

'You did send all those people out to the house just to annoy me, didn't you?' she asked.

Price nodded, his eyes now brimming with laughter. 'I knew sooner or later it would bring you to me.'

This time it was Amanda's turn to flush as she remembered the day she went to Price's office to complain and the night that followed.

Price sobered as he too recalled the events of that night. After a prolonged silence he said, 'Amanda, I'm sorry about the way I treated you. Things should have been different between us. I was shocked to discover you were still a virgin. Who would have guessed? Especially at your age.'

Thanks so much for mentioning that. She could feel her cheeks grow hot and ordinarily she would have offered some witty comeback except that he was right. Who would have guessed?

'I didn't know how to deal with you.' Price's voice was husky now. 'Why did you do it, Amanda? Why did you let me make love to you?'

Already embarrassed by this whole conversation, Amanda shrugged her shoulders and replied with an attempt at humour. 'As you just pointed out, it was about time, don't you think?'

Price reached across the table and took her hand in his. 'No,' he said, 'I have to know.'

'Please don't,' she whispered. 'Don't make me answer that.'

Price considered her request and didn't push her for an

answer. There would be another time. Instead, he directed their conversation to a lighter subject.

The candle on the table flickered, accentuating the strong planes of Price's face, the same face that had haunted her dreams each night. She knew with certainty that she was in love with him. Maybe she had always loved him, since the first time she had laid eyes on him that summer, so long ago.

Hers had been the crush of a very young girl for an older man – he was all of twenty-one then and she was fifteen. At fifteen, she had reasoned that six years wasn't such a huge difference in age. He could wait for her to become a woman, to catch up. She didn't understand that, at twenty-one, he had had no concept of her and the woman she would become. To him, she was a child. His sights were set on a distant horizon, and this was only one summer in a lifetime of summers.

Following the death of her father, and what later came to be abandonment by her mother, Amanda had soaked up the teasing, playful attention of both Bobby and Price, even though much of it came from their efforts to ditch the two teenaged girls who had made a game of shadowing their every move. Bobby's sister also had a crush on Price. She got over it, but Amanda never did.

They lingered at the table long after dinner was over, savouring the interlude, and with each word, each phrase, Amanda forgot that what she wanted, Price was unwilling to share on a permanent basis. When they left the restaurant, they were immediately surrounded by the soft, seductive perfume of the honeysuckle that grew all around. The air was still and warm, a night for lovers.

As they drove through the darkness, he reached out to her, lightly caressing the back of her neck, playing with the silky strands of hair that rested against her shoulders. His touch was so gentle that Amanda forgot to be on guard.

Pulling into the parking space next to her car, Price turned off the ignition and in one fluid motion he leaned toward her and gathered her to him. Softly, quietly, his lips brushed hers, and under this non-aggressive assault, her lips gently caressed his in return. Without a sound, Amanda told him that she cared. Without words, she told him that she loved him.

Price's lips wandered to the soft place where her jaw swept up to meet her ear. He inhaled deeply. The smell of her skin was sweet and somehow new. She was new, he reflected, not practised in her responses to him, still shy and tentative until he would do the things to her that would release her hidden passion.

'So sweet,' he whispered against her hair. 'Amanda, honey, I don't want to leave you. I need you, but I can't continue this in the car either. Leave your car here and I'll bring you back to get it in the morning.' Until that moment, Amanda had been enveloped in the soft mist of his warmth and affection, hoping that her love might be in some measure returned. Only his whispered words served to shatter her illusions. propelling her into icy reality.

How could I be so stupid? It was a silent scream. He only wanted her for the night, just like before. This man was more dangerous to her than anyone or anything had ever been. By the power of his presence and his caresses, he had made her believe that he was returning the love she had for him. And she had wanted so badly to believe that he cared for her, that she had allowed herself to be duped. Again.

For her, there had to be something more. Slowly, she unlocked her arms from around his neck and let her hands skim his shoulders down to his strong, sinewy arms. Bracing her hands finally against his chest, she brought her eyes up to meet his searching gaze.

Price knew what she was about to say. He could read it

in her eyes. He saw regret, and anger. He saw sadness and, disturbingly, disappointment. She lowered her eyes and rested her forehead against his hard chest. Slowly, deliberately, she moved her head from side-to-side. Then without looking at him again, she pulled away and opened the car door, then hurried over to her own car. Quickly, she started the engine and drove out of the parking lot.

Price was furious. He knew why she had left him. He had seen it in her eyes when she had looked up at him in sadness. But he was not only furious with her, he was furious with himself. Amanda was disappointed in him. She wanted him to say that he cared for her, that he had felt the love she had for him in the kisses they shared. Price had felt it and was thrilled by it, but he wasn't ready to respond. He had set up powerful barriers in defence of the effect she had on him, barriers that didn't fall easily.

For long moments, he sat in his car staring into the blackness and seeing only Amanda's face. Suddenly he turned the key in the ignition, threw the car into reverse, then into drive. The tires screeched against the pavement as he pulled out on to the deserted street. As he drove he pulled at his tie, loosening it then discarding it. Then he unfastened the top buttons of his shirt and shrugged out of his suit jacket. Once more he remembered the look on Amanda's face. *She may have a switch she can turn from hot to cold*, he thought, *but I don't*!

He pulled up in front of the house just as Amanda was turning off the lights. He jumped from his car and ran up the steps and pounded on the door. She opened the door only a few inches. Price caught the door and pushed it open with such force that Amanda lost her balance and stumbled backward. He grabbed her by the shoulders pulling her close and wrapping his arms around her. His strong hands moved up and down from her shoulders to her buttocks, fitting her to the contours of his aroused body.

Even as disillusioned as she was with what had happened earlier, her resistance crumbled in the face of his undisguised desire and his blatant sensuality. Nor could she bring herself to push him away, or even utter the single word that she knew would have stopped him. Desire flared, ignited, and soon became a consuming, raging blaze that left her helpless and begging to be satisfied.

As if in answer, his hands moved over her roughly as his mouth savoured the sweetness of hers. Her passion followed his lead from one plateau to another. The need for the touch and taste of one another caused them to frantically tear at the clothing that acted as barriers between them, ripping at each scrap, then tossing them away. This time there was no lazy seduction, only a heated frenzy as they lay on the floor, bodies intertwined in the midst of discarded clothing and packing boxes that stood like silent sentries.

As his eyes slid to her breasts, now covered with the satin sheen of moonlight from the windows, he was stunned at his overwhelming need to claim her completely. Amanda didn't flinch as she met his dark blue eyes, instead she went on to satisfy her need to run her hands over his aroused body. Frantically and powerfully, their bodies met over and over in a fury of desire that neither one had ever experienced. As they moved together in this most elemental expression of love, Price knew unequivocally that this act was to mark him for the rest of his life. This time he could not walk away from her.

Still breathing heavily, he moved his hands to each side of the fragile and beautiful face before him. Brushing damp tendrils of hair from her forehead, he kissed her lightly on her lips. 'You do things to me that I don't even think you're aware of.'

She smiled and whispered back to him, 'That's what you get for turning me into a shameful, wanton creature.'

Slowly, Price rolled to his side pulling Amanda with him. 'Do you think that next time you could control yourself long enough to get to the bedroom?'

She smiled, and it was the smile of a satisfied woman – a woman in love.

Amanda stretched and opened her eyes to the morning light. Memories of the night before came rushing back and she smiled contentedly. She hadn't any other experiences for comparison, but she was sure that Price was a wonderful lover. He was passionate and considerate, rough and gentle, and the tempo of their night together had been a symphony of pleasure. From the sounds below, Amanda assumed that Price was downstairs in the kitchen. She decided to take a quick shower before joining him.

When she stepped out of the bathroom, the tantalising smell of freshly-brewed coffee greeted her. She tied the belt of her robe and ran a comb through her hair before she ran down the stairs to join him.

He was facing the stove against the far wall, unaware that Amanda had entered the kitchen. Quickly she walked across the room and wrapped her arms around him, her breasts pressing against his naked back.

'That's dangerous, Miss Hamilton,' he laughed. 'You may never get breakfast. But I could promise you something hot in the kitchen.'

Her face turned red at the prospect and she took a step back as he turned toward her. He was dressed only in a pair of pants. His chest and feet were bare and she couldn't keep her eyes off him.

Over coffee, they lingered at the kitchen table, each reluctant to break the spell between them. Finally Price looked at his watch and realised that it was getting late. 'I have to go. I'm leaving town on business in a few hours. Will you meet me here Friday evening?'

Amanda nodded. 'I'll be nearly finished with everything by then.'

Price looked around. 'I wish I were going to be here to help you with all this,' he said, indicating the stacks of boxes that filled every vacant space.

'I'll manage,' she said, 'until you get back.'

'You could stay, you know.'

There it was, the invitation. So tempting, so easy, so wrong for her. 'Thank you,' she said, 'but this house belongs to you now. I need to find my own way and I can't do that if I stay here.'

When he had put on his shirt, she walked with him to his car. He leaned down to kiss her, a lover's kiss followed by a light touch and a whispered goodbye.

The rest of the day passed in a daze. Caught somewhere between reality and fantasy, Amanda could only think of the night they had shared and dream of what might be ahead. Every so often, she would pause, pick up a few items, place them in a carton, then lapse once more into her dreamlike state. The movers were due on Thursday and she knew she should finish the last minute packing. Finally, she abandoned all attempts at working. Tomorrow was soon enough.

Today was hers for dreaming.

chapter seven

Thursday morning dawned bright and crisp. Amanda awakened early, ready to finish the tasks she had put off. Even though moving to her new apartment in town was uppermost in her mind, she still had difficulty coming to terms with the fact that this house was no longer hers. It belonged to Price now. She sighed as she looked around. At least he had promised he would take care of the place. She had to take comfort from that. It was hard to leave this haven, but the memories of her years here belonged to her. Nothing could take them away. Now she was about to make a new start.

There were only two boxes left to be labelled and sealed when she heard a car drive up. Looking out the window, she was surprised to see it was Joan.

'What are you doing here?' Amanda asked when Joan stepped inside and leaned breathlessly against the door frame. 'Don't you have to work today?'

'I *was* working today,' replied Joan, waving a magazine in her hand, 'until I saw this. I was going to call you but I knew you wouldn't be able to get hold of a copy of this right away. So, I decided to take the rest of the day off. Oh, Amanda, I bet you don't know anything at all about this and I...'

Amanda smiled. 'Joan, take a deep breath and calm down. What are you talking about? What could be important enough for you to drive all the way out here in the middle of the afternoon?'

They made their way from the front door to the kitchen. Joan slumped into a chair at the kitchen table and dramatically slammed the latest issue of 'Business Today' on the table.

Amanda reached for the magazine, her hand stopping in mid air as she recognised the incredibly handsome face staring back at her from the front cover. 'It's Price! Oh my gosh!' She laughed nervously. 'What's so bad about this? He's a celebrity!'

'That's what I thought too. Sit down and read.'

Amanda flipped the pages until she reached the feature article about Price. She began to read, then stopped. Looking up at Joan she said, 'I don't see that this is anything to be upset about. I'm impressed. I knew he was successful, but I had no idea he was worth this kind of money.'

'*Made* that kind of money, Amanda, in less than six years. Keep reading.'

Amanda looked at the glossy pages of the magazine spread out before her. There was a picture of Price at a construction site, one of a completed residential development, and another of him in his office with Caroline Sloan. The caption under the photo identified her as his partner. Amanda resumed reading.

The meteoric rise of architect and real estate developer Price McCord is due largely to his innovative concept of real estate development for the 'Over 50' market. Often identified as 'empty nesters', this market had largely been ignored by developers as a recognisable economic force in the home building industry. While others assumed that down-sizing, often into a condo or smaller home, was the next step, only McCord recognised that with the kids no longer a drain on their finances, many couples were finally ready to build their dream homes – their big dream homes – the ones that practically shouted out their success.

Cumberland River, McCord & Company's largest development to date, skyrocketed McCord, 32, and his partner, interior designer Caroline Sloan, 27, into the ranks of the million-dollar babies.

The article went on to describe how Price and Caroline developed and marketed their beautiful homes and the concept of the Cumberland River project. Cumberland itself was the name of a Civil War-era plantation located in the coastal region of South Carolina. First, they restored the house, which had been built in 1856, to its original beauty, then used it as the anchor, much like a country club, for all the other homes that were built around it.

These homes were large, filled with unexpected luxury, located in a naturally beautiful setting enhanced with walkways, ponds, unexpected flower gardens and, of course, tennis courts, swimming pools and a championship golf course. The theory behind this development and the reason for its overwhelming success was simple: Cumberland River gave the 'Over 50' group a chance to enjoy a carefree lifestyle, yet offered them the kind of luxury homes that reflected their obvious success.

Amanda was speechless. She continued to read:

'I searched for a long time before I found the Cumberland house,' said McCord. 'When I first saw it, I was impressed by its stately beauty. Then I was amazed by its state of disrepair. But since it was perfect for what I had in mind, the cost of restoration was worth it.'

And what does the imaginative team of McCord and Sloan have in mind next?

'I've already located the house and the site for my next development. The plans are ready. I'm just waiting for the former owner to vacate the premises. Once that's done, Caroline and I will get down to work.'

Amanda was in shock. Her house! This was why he had bought her house! It was perfect for his purposes. Price was going to fix up the house and turn it into a country club. He would build expensive homes on the surrounding fifty acres and turn it into another development like Cumberland River. He had lied to her. He never intended to live here.

Jumping up, Amanda threw the magazine across the room in a fury. 'I won't let him do this!' she cried. Her voice was shaking with uncontrollable emotion, part-anger, part-hurt. 'How could he lie to me like that? How could he be so devious? I'm not going to let him get away with this. I'll stop him!'

'Amanda, this isn't your house anymore,' said Joan. 'You signed the papers two days ago. I only wish I had seen a copy of the magazine earlier.'

'He is not going to get away with this,' repeated Amanda. 'Joan, do you know a lawyer?'

'I don't think a lawyer is going to be able to help you. Just be glad that you didn't get seriously involved with him. Any man who would pull a stunt like this is a liar and a cheat.'

Amanda rolled her eyes toward the ceiling as if seeking heavenly intervention. 'I did, Joan,' said Amanda, the hurt obvious in her voice.

'You did what?' asked Joan.

Amanda waved her hand through the air in a gesture that signalled frustration. 'Involved. You might as well know – I slept with Price. He really got to me, Joan, and I let him.'

'Is it serious?'

'It was, until now. I can't believe I waited so damn long to fall in love only to be duped. Give me the name of the lawyer, Joan.'

Amanda spent the rest of the afternoon on the phone. She soon found out that legally she had no recourse. As soon as she had sold the house, she had relinquished all rights to it. Morally, what Price had done, advised the lawyer, was no worse than what happened after thousands of other real estate transactions. A buyer did not have to disclose what he planned to do with the property he was buying.

Amanda hung up, still undaunted. There had to be another way. Next she called the County Commissioner's office. While Price had not filed any papers to have the property re-zoned, she learned that because of the existing agricultural designation it might not be necessary. For the next hour, Amanda grabbed at anything she could think of that might present a stumbling block to keep him from proceeding with his plans.

By dinnertime, she had to admit to Joan that she had been right all along. She had no control whatsoever over the fate of her house. In an effort to console her, Joan took Amanda out for a quiet dinner. For someone who had lost so much in her life, it seemed to Joan that Amanda was destined to lose much more. She deserved better.

Later when she was alone, Amanda finally had to face facts. She wanted to label Price a liar, a man who bought her house under false pretences, but the truth was that he had not lied to her. It had never occurred to her to ask him what plans he had for the house. She had assumed that he would live in it, just as she had. And he had paid the full asking price, so she had no complaints there.

She had been a fool to think that Price cared for her. Had he been laughing at her all along? How could her instincts about him have been so wrong? She asked herself this question and others, and realised that all along she had known he was dangerous, yet she had fallen in love with him. Amanda just never suspected that he would take something she loved so dearly and turn it into something it should never be. Once again, she was disillusioned and disappointed.

'Ladies and gentlemen,' said the flight attendant, 'we will soon begin our approach to Atlanta's Hartsfield International Airport. Please fasten your seat belts and return your seats to the upright position. The temperature in Atlanta is 82 degrees. The time is four o'clock pm. We shall be landing in about 15 minutes. On behalf of the captain and crew, I would like to thank you for flying with us. We hope you enjoy your stay in Atlanta.'

Price adjusted his seat. He was glad to be back. Even though he had been gone only two days, the trip had been strenuous and negotiations had not gone smoothly. Bothered by the need to make a decision about his involvement with Amanda, his concentration wavered. He knew she would not be content to drift along with things as they were.

Strange, he thought as he gazed out of the window and watched the clouds give way to the landscape below, *of all the women I've known, not one has ever made me feel the need to define a relationship, nor have I ever felt the need to take action of any kind. Except in the case of Shelley*, he amended. But that was an altogether different situation – a time in his life too painful to remember.

The thought of marriage had been a recurring disturbance during this trip. Most of his relationships had just drifted along with one or the other person finally losing interest. Amanda affected Price deeply. He had been startled by the intensity of his need for her. Not given to introspection where women were concerned, it annoyed him that he hadn't been able to put thoughts of her aside. It also bothered him that she had made her feelings for him so obvious. When he hadn't been able to mask his responses to her, he had felt as if he were losing control of his destiny, a difficulty for a man who had built his success by planning and exercising control over each step of his future.

As planned, Amanda drove from her new apartment out to the house to meet him. Ever since she found out about his plan to turn her house into a development, she had vacillated between anger, hurt, hostility and, surprisingly, the need to see him again. In her mind, she had acted out the scenario a million times. What she would say, what he would say? In fact, she had no idea what she was going to do or say to him now that the moment had arrived.

It was still early as she let herself into the empty house to wait for him. Being alone at dusk had always made her sad – it was the time of day when she felt most alone. Today, she felt it more than ever.

Price drove up only a few minutes later, relieved to see that Amanda was already there. In the few hours since he had returned, his need to see her, to talk to her, had accelerated. He found her in the kitchen, and he halted as he entered the room. She was sitting on the kitchen counter dressed in a long skirt and blouse. The fabric was splattered with soft watercolour pastels against a cream background. Her sandaled feet, crossed at the ankles, were swinging back and forth impatiently.

Suddenly she was still, holding her breath, waiting. She had known when Price had entered the house. What she hadn't known was how breathtaking it would be to see him again. Time and motion were suspended for each of them. The tension in the room was palatable.

Expelling the breath she had been holding, Amanda was the first to break the spell. Lightly swinging her feet again, she set time in motion once more and returned the order of things to the way they should be. 'Hello, Price,' she said in a low voice.

Price crossed the room toward her. 'I've missed you.'

Amanda held up her hand to halt his forward progress then slid off the counter, the slit in her skirt riding high on her thigh.

Price's eyes followed the path of her skirt, lingering there appreciatively. He took another step toward her.

'Don't come any closer,' she said. 'I'm only here to

make you an offer. I want to buy this house back from you.'

Lowering his brows, Price scrutinised Amanda. His eyes clouded. He certainly hadn't expected this. He stood silently, watching her. Then, raising his brow slightly, he said in an impersonal voice, 'Would you care to elaborate?'

Amanda glanced down quickly as if by doing so she could arm herself against him. Then she raised her eyes and her chin defiantly. 'I've made a mistake in selling this house to you. I grew up here, Price. There are too many memories. I thought I could live somewhere else but I can't.'

Price slowly retreated to the other side of the kitchen. Casually, he arranged his long frame against the cabinets, his arms folded across his chest. 'And?' he prompted.

'That's all,' she answered. 'I just want to buy the house back.'

Price knew that there had to be other reasons for the sudden change of heart. He tried not to think of his disappointment at her reaction to seeing him again. Once more there were barriers between them and he wanted to know what had brought on the sudden change. 'What's your offer?' he asked in a low voice.

'It's the same as what yours was to me. I'll give you exactly what you paid for the house, and you give me back the house.' She had decided she would do whatever she had to to get it back – even if it meant asking Sam to make her a loan.

Behind his unreadable expression, Price was experiencing a kind of perverse pleasure. He was discovering that it was infinitely more pleasurable to have something that Amanda wanted instead of wanting something from her. 'Not good enough,' he said. 'The price has gone up.'

'Gone up?' Amanda choked on the words. 'You've only had this house for a few days and you have the nerve to tell me that the price has gone up? Does this have something to do with your newest real estate venture?'

Now he knew what had brought all this on. Amanda must have seen the article in 'Business Today', and putting two and two together, figured this house was to be the site of his new development. In the very beginning, he had considered it, but when he found another tract of land closer to the city he ruled this one out. The location wasn't right. While it was true that the house itself would have made an ideal setting, it was also true that it was just too rural, too far away from things like grocery stores and shopping centres and too far to commute to work.

Amanda continued, this time in a more personal vein. 'Did you enjoy the time we spent together while you were planning all along to take the house I love and turn it into another Cumberland River? Was I part of the acquisition...just a perk you hadn't counted on?' Amanda spat out the words, each one cutting and more bitter than the ones before. 'I imagine you and Caroline had quite a laugh over this. Tell me, Price, does she know you got some action on the side, or is she the kind who wouldn't care?'

'Stick to the subject, Amanda,' Price said in a low, hard voice. 'What happened between us was private. It had nothing to do with anyone else.'

'I don't have any more money, as you have probably guessed, and you paid the full asking price. The house isn't worth any more than that and you know it.' The bitterness that Amanda harboured spilled over.

Price didn't bother to correct her assumption that this house was to be the site of his next development. And it was obvious that Amanda would have never sold it if she hadn't been in dire financial circumstances. She loved it too much. He also neglected to correct her assumption that Caroline was his lover. The magazine article had identified them only as business partners. It made no mention of the fact that they were also brother and sister.

In spite of her hostility, he still wanted her. Price studied Amanda intently as he thought over the turn that events had taken. He knew he held all the cards. Amanda wanted her house back. The reason was immaterial – he could now bargain with her. Suddenly he swore under his breath. What the hell was he thinking of?

Just hours ago, he was feeling compelled to make a decision about their relationship. Now he wanted to see how far she would go to get her house back. While he knew that it was wrong of him to toy with her like this, nevertheless, he had an overwhelming desire to know what kind of power he could exercise over her. He was hurt by her lack of trust. He wanted to strike back.

Curtly he said, 'If you want the house badly enough, we can come to some sort of agreement.'

'How? I've told you what I can pay and you've already refused.'

'There are other things to bargain with besides money,' he answered. Carefully he watched for her reaction.

There was a pause then her eyes widened and her hand flew to her lips as she realised the true meaning behind his words. She had never for a minute considered that he would resort to this age-old method of bargaining between men and women. 'You're not serious!' she hissed.

'I am,' he replied with amusement from across the room.

'You are disgusting! How could you even think that I would go along with something like that?' she cried.

'I didn't think about it at all,' Price said. 'It just seemed to fit this particular situation. We both get something we want.'

'No,' she said.

'I'm open to a counter-proposal,' he said with a smile.

'Don't you mean a counter-proposition?' she said bitterly.

Price shrugged and settled himself more comfortably against the kitchen cabinet. 'Call it whatever you like.'

Amanda was ready to launch a scathing verbal attack that would, among other things, seriously question his ancestry, when Price pushed himself away from the counter and slowly crossed the kitchen toward her. As he approached, she reached to retrieve her bag from the counter behind her. Turning back, she was surprised to find him in front of her. Within seconds, he had pinned her hips to the cabinet behind her with the pressure of his. His hands rested on either side of her. Trapped, she watched him warily, her anger barely controlled.

Price searched her face intently. 'Doesn't the night we spent together right here in this house mean anything to you?'

'I'm leaving,' Amanda said in a tight voice. 'I'm not going to let you make a fool of me any longer.'

'Not yet,' he ordered.

She could feel the temperature in the kitchen rising. She had to get away. 'Let me go, Price. Just stay away from me. I want nothing more to do with you.'

'Do you mean that?' he asked.

'Yes,' she answered coldly. 'I do. I wish I had never met you. You're not someone I can trust.'

Price stepped back immediately, severing all physical contact, then he turned and walked out of the kitchen and into the living room. Amanda remained where she was for a moment longer, certain she would never see him or the inside of this house again. She bit her lip to keep from crying as she rushed through the hallway and out of the front door.

He watched from the window as she got into her car and drove off. He stood there for a long time, staring into the darkness before he realised that his hurt had turned to a cold, hard resolve.

Price worked late into the night. It was his one defence against what he had been feeling since the last time he had seen Amanda. He had fought the urge to see her again, to call her. Most of all, he cursed himself for being foolish enough to have backed her into a corner without leaving her a way out. Angrily, he ran his hand through his hair and down to the base of his taut neck.

He should have told her the truth that he had no plans for the house other than to live in it. Maybe it would have made a difference. But she had assumed the worst about him and had never even gave him a chance to explain. He was hurt and angry at the way she had treated him but, most of all, he was surprised that it mattered so much.

Price shook his head. He had been lulled into feeling remorseful by the lateness of the hour. He stood, turned out the lights and locked the door and wished he could lock out thoughts of Amanda that easily.

Walking away from Price had been the hardest thing Amanda had ever done, but this time she had refused to grieve over him. The days slipped by, some more easily than others. She made a real effort to expand her horizons by exploring her new neighbourhood. Already she had met many of her neighbours and some of the shop owners.

Summer was only a memory as November arrived and the beauty of autumn began to wane. Amanda refused to think of Price. It was too painful and debilitating. Once she had even driven out to the house then, before she reached the last turn that would take her down the long tree-lined drive, she had turned around.

It didn't matter anymore. That part of her life was over.

chapter eight

She slammed the door to her apartment with such violence that the walls shuddered. Amanda reached down to remove one shoe, then grabbed for the other. Standing barefoot in her living room she threw them across the room as hard as she could – each shoe in turn accompanied with a curse.

No one had been more startled than Amanda when the doctor had told her she was pregnant. Almost two-and-a-half months, he had said. Had she even suspected, she could have saved herself a lot of trouble – they have tests at the chemist! She could have also saved herself a lot of embarrassment – she had burst into tears in his office. But she didn't suspect anything at all.

'How could I be so damn stupid?' she shouted into the empty apartment. 'There is absolutely not one single reason for a woman my age to find themselves in this awful predicament! Just what on earth am I supposed to do now?' Amanda stomped over to the sofa and flopped down, grabbing a pillow and hugging it in front of her. 'This is a dirty, rotten trick,' she said as she began to cry again.

Much later, when the tears would no longer come, Amanda pulled herself off the sofa and went into the kitchen to fix a cup of tea. She was shaking and uncoordinated as she put a kettle on to boil, almost as if her bout of tears had robbed her of the ability to perform even the most ordinary of tasks.

Carrying the steaming tea back to the living room a few minutes later, she settled back on to the sofa. Now that she was calmer, she needed to sit quietly and think things through. She mustn't panic.

Why hadn't she known? She had been busy first with moving, then with fixing up the apartment, then with illustrations for a new book, the list went on. Plus, her symptoms had been much like the flu she had last winter. She had lost weight, she was having trouble keeping food down, and she was sleepy much of the time. She never even realised that she had missed the most obvious sign of all because her cycle was often irregular.

She rubbed her eyes with the heels of her hands. Counting back, she knew that it had happened the night they had closed on the house, the night Price had made love to her on the living room floor.

I've got to think this thing through logically. After all, there are options, she thought. But when she reviewed them they all seemed to disappear. She was going to have a baby!

With each day that passed, she began to feel different. Physically her symptoms remained much the same. But emotionally she began to accept that what was happening to her was the beginning of a new life and, like it or not, she had been appointed caretaker. Amanda guarded her secret, unwilling to share it with anyone – not with Joan and definitely not with Price. A man who couldn't commit to a relationship certainly couldn't commit to the responsibility that fatherhood would entail.

Caroline was acutely aware that Price's behaviour at the office was the subject of many morning and afternoon coffee breaks, and that he did nothing whatsoever to counteract the speculation that was rampant among their employees. He was sullen, uncommunicative, and when forced to interact with his staff, he was brief and to the point.

He had also ceased to see anyone socially, including his own family. When things had deteriorated to a point where she could stand it no longer, Caroline decided to confront her brother and get to the bottom of things.

As usual, her husband, Mike, had warned her to stay out of it. As usual, she ignored his advice. Caroline knew Amanda was responsible for Price's state of mind. Secretly she applauded this woman – the first since Shelley – to affect her brother in this way. However, dealing with Price's disposition every day was in no way a laughing matter.

A few days later, Caroline coaxed her brother into joining her for lunch at one of their favourite places, hoping he would relax and open up to her. As soon as they ordered, Caroline assumed a relaxed pose and carefully broached the subject.

Price smiled at her, then after a few minutes he caught on to her intent and laughed wryly. 'Caroline, I know you too well. You've planned this chummy little lunch so that you can interrogate me. I've never heard you make such a sly attempt at diplomacy – plus a free lunch – just so you can wheedle information out of me. It just isn't your style, so why don't you get on with what you want to know. You're going to ask me anyway.'

'Oh, damn. Was I that bad? No wonder I have such a hard time getting Mike to tell me stuff. I just want to know what's wrong, why you've been so moody and so difficult to get along with and…,' said Caroline with an impish smile on her face, '…I want to know the identity of the woman responsible.'

Price couldn't help but laugh. His sister didn't know the meaning of the word 'subtle'.

'There is no woman, Caroline. I'm just wrestling with some decisions I need to make. Besides, you know how much time and energy I've put into this new project. It's got to be right before we can go ahead.'

Caroline looked him straight in the eye. 'I don't believe you.'

Price raised his eyebrows.

'You're in the shape you're in because, dear brother, some woman has finally got to you. Imagine that,' she said to the restaurant at large, 'my oh-so-cool-brother, man-about-town, perennial bachelor, is in love.'

Price's smile quickly disappeared and was replaced with an expression that would have deterred many people from going any further. But not Caroline. She knew that she was right and she wasn't about to give up now.

'It's time you faced up to the facts of life, just like everyone else. The truth is that Price McCord is just as vulnerable as the rest of us. You've finally realised that maybe, just maybe, you can't be happy without someone to share that happiness. But I'll bet you're not prepared to make that kind of commitment. To you, that would equate with admitting that your life so far has been pretty empty. Well Price, in my opinion, it has. Some people never get a chance at true happiness. They never meet the right person.' Caroline drew a deep breath and plunged ahead. 'You're lucky – you've found Amanda Hamilton.'

Price's expression hardened. Caroline surprised him, and her assessment made him uneasy. It was too near the truth.

'Amanda Hamilton had a house for sale, Caroline, and I decided to buy it. The deal is closed – end of story. And if you don't change the subject, this will be the end of our lunch.'

'But Price,' she said in an attempt to find out something more, 'I was with you at the club that night, remember? I saw how you reacted to her and I saw the two of you on the dance floor.' Caroline took a deep breath then plunged ahead. 'Surely you can't deny that you feel something for her?'

'Caroline...' he said in a warning tone that wouldn't allow any further comment.

Quickly she changed the subject, but her mind raced on. She was right. She knew it all along. Price would have never reacted that way if she hadn't been right on target about Amanda. Even as they were finishing lunch, Caroline was plotting her next move. Somehow she would find a way to get Price and Amanda together.

The wastepaper basket overflowed with crumpled sheets of paper. Amanda was having trouble with her latest assignment, and she was becoming increasingly frustrated by her attempts to draw the same thing over and over. Glancing at her watch, she saw that it was nearly noon and so far she hadn't accomplished anything. Maybe a break and some lunch would help.

She was still having trouble keeping food down, but the doctor assured her that this phase would soon pass. *If I don't die first*, she thought. Stretching, she rose from the chair and stacked all the sketches that hadn't been condemned to the wastepaper basket in a neat pile.

In the kitchen, she filled the kettle and turned on the front burner on the stove. She was unenthusiastically surveying the contents of her fridge when she heard the doorbell ring. She hurried to answer it and was surprised to find Caroline Sloan standing there. *Good God. What next?* Her day was not going well at all – and now this! What could she possibly want? And what was it with this woman that she kept popping up at the most inconvenient times? How had she even known where to find her?

This time, Caroline waited to be invited in, her attitude vastly different from their first meeting. 'Hi, Amanda, remember me? Caroline Sloan. I was at your house a few months ago before you sold it to Price McCord.'

How could I possibly forget? 'I remember,' said

Amanda, inwardly groaning as she recalled that fateful day along with her uncharacteristic rudeness to Caroline. She surveyed her visitor then reluctantly stepped aside. 'Come on in. I was just about to have some tea. Would you care for some?' Amanda signalled for Caroline to follow her.

'Thank you, that would be nice.'

Amanda poured the steaming tea into two cups then carried them to the table.

'I know you're wondering why I'm here,' said Caroline when they were seated. 'I'm very concerned about Price and, to come straight to the point, I believe you might have caused his current condition.'

Caroline's candour caught Amanda off guard. *Just as he is for mine*, thought Amanda ironically. Out loud she asked, 'Which is?'

'Rotten,' answered Caroline. 'He shuts himself away in his office every day under the guise of working. He's sullen and impossible to get along with. In short, he's miserable.'

'And you think I'm responsible for this?' Amanda asked, the inquiry laced with humour as well as sarcasm. 'I haven't seen Price for quite some time. While in a perverse sort of way it's almost flattering that you think I could have done this to him, I can assure you, Caroline, I'm not the cause.' *I only wish I was.*

Amanda took a deep breath. This was the perfect time to address the relationship between Price and Caroline. 'If Price's current state of mind is making you miserable and interfering with your business, that's something you will have to deal with the best way you can. After all, you and Price were involved with one another long before I met him.'

Caroline sipped her tea, her eyes meeting Amanda's over the rim of her cup. 'What do you mean "involved"?' she asked curiously.

'I mean you had a relationship, or whatever you choose to call it. Now if...' Amanda started to rise but Caroline reached out a hand to restrain her.

'Amanda, please,' said Caroline. 'Sit down for a moment. I need to clarify something. Are you saying that you think Price and I are a couple?'

Amanda nodded.

'What makes you think that?'

'Well, you're business partners. And when I asked Price about where you fit in the picture and your personal relationship with him, he didn't deny it.'

Caroline shook her head in disbelief. 'What a rotten thing for him to do! He let you believe that we were...? Good heavens, Amanda, Price is my brother.'

Amanda's eyes widened and with a startled look on her face she repeated, 'Your brother?'

Caroline nodded affirmatively.

'Your brother? Why that lying so-and-so...!'

'Yes,' said Caroline, grinning. 'My thoughts exactly. He's always telling me that I shouldn't meddle in his affairs, but in spite of what I think of him right at this moment, it looks as if one of you needs a push in the right direction.'

Amanda was silent for a moment trying to digest this surprising piece of information. 'I see. I...' Amanda was startled by the shrill ring of the phone. 'Excuse me,' she mumbled as she got up to answer the phone that hung on the wall above the kitchen counter.

While waiting for her to return to the table, Caroline glanced idly at the stack of mail in the centre of the kitchen table. Her eyes strayed to the card on top. She read it almost without thinking, then quickly reread it.

It was a standard card used by many doctors to remind patients of their appointments, but this card was from the office of an obstetrician and it clearly was a reminder for Amanda's three-month pre-natal appointment.

Pre-natal? Amanda was pregnant? Caroline did a quick calculation backwards and determined that it was about two-and-a-half months ago when Price had bought Amanda's house. Had he been seeing Amanda then? She couldn't be sure, but she recalled the two of them dancing that night at the club. That had to be it! But did Price know about this? Was that why he was so miserable? No, he couldn't know…he would never ignore his responsibilities. For a moment, she thought about Shelley and she knew her brother would do the right thing.

Caroline was positive about two things and both were based on nothing more than instinct. One was that this baby belonged to Price. The other was that Amanda had never told Price that she was pregnant. But why? Surely he was in love with her. And how could Amanda not be in love with him? But then Caroline remembered that they hadn't seen each other for quite some time – not since the sale of the house. Something must have gone wrong between them. Without any qualms, Caroline took the appointment card and slipped it into her bag.

When Amanda returned to the table, Caroline stood and extended her hand. 'I have to go. Please get in touch with Price, I think he needs you and is too stubborn to tell you so.'

'Thank you, Caroline. I know your concern for him is genuine, but there is absolutely nothing between us.'
Except a baby.

As she drove away from Amanda's apartment building, Caroline realised that she was no closer to bringing Price and Amanda together than she was before. Only now, there was a real urgency. Quickly she checked the side mirror and the rear view mirror, then made a sharp U-turn. She had to talk to Price right away.

After Caroline left, Amanda tried to go back to work, but the apartment felt claustrophobic. She missed her old place so much that sometimes it hurt. The tranquillity and peace she had felt there had been replaced by the muted sounds of a city neighbourhood, not altogether unpleasant, but different. And even though the area was quiet during the week except for the morning sounds of residents as they left for work and then returned home, it was bustling on the weekends. Just another adjustment she had to make. She had done her best here, turning the dining room into her studio, but it was too small, too confining, and the closest thing she had to a view from her drawing board was her neighbour's porch and the trees beyond. Maybe a long walk would help her put things into perspective.

Today the air was crisp but not cold, so Amanda donned a heavy sweater instead of a coat. As she walked at a slower pace than usual, she breathed deeply trying to still the panic that had been triggered by Caroline's revelation. After she had gone a few blocks, she calmed down enough to consider the implications of what Price's sister had told her.

In her mind, she replayed their conversation in detail. It wasn't any consolation to know that Price was unhappy. She wasn't happy either, but now she had a baby to think of. For her, there was never any option other than having this baby. Once she had got over the initial shock, she realised she wanted someone in her life to love.

Amanda had been completely stunned to learn that Caroline and Price were brother and sister. There was absolutely no family resemblance. And while she was relieved to know that Caroline was Price's sister, she was also saddened by it. It only served to point toward his refusal to engage in a committed relationship. It wasn't because he was involved with Caroline as Amanda had thought – it was simply that he didn't want a relationship with her.

She sighed and pushed her hands deep into the pockets of her jeans. It didn't do any good to be angry. She had to concentrate on the positive things in her life. She had someone else to think about now.

chapter nine

Price joined Caroline in his living room. 'OK, what's so important that you had to rush right over and invade my privacy?' He plopped down on the sofa and stretched his long legs out in front of him, resigned to a session with his sister.

Ignoring his sarcasm, Caroline silently acknowledged that Amanda's spontaneous and colourful assessment of her brother's character was one hundred per cent correct. Now she surveyed him with a patience she didn't know she had, waiting until he was comfortably settled before she spoke. He had just showered and his dark hair was still damp. His shirt was unbuttoned and his jeans hugged his thighs.

'Price,' she said softly, 'I know you told me to mind my own business, but I have to talk to you again about Amanda.' Caroline held her breath for a moment as she waited to gauge his reaction.

'What about her?' Price asked. He was surprised that she had decided to bring up Amanda's name again after their last conversation. He waited, maintaining his lazy demeanour, confident that the less importance he gave to this conversation, the sooner he could get rid of Caroline.

She didn't respond. Instead she reached into her purse for the card she had taken from Amanda's table. She held it delicately between her fingertips, her expression serious, knowing that the information on this card would cause Price to make a major change in his life. Then she handed it to him.

He reached for it, his blue eyes first wide and curious,

then narrowing into slits of steel as he read and reread the card.

Silently, Caroline watched.

'Where did you get this?' he asked in a low, tightly controlled voice.

'I went to see her today.'

'Why?' he questioned tersely.

'Because I was convinced that she...that you and her...something happened between you and I just wanted to talk to her,' Caroline finished lamely.

'And did she confirm your theory?'

'No. She said she hadn't seen you for quite some time, since the sale of the house, and that there was nothing between the two of you. She, uh, had a phone call while I was there, and I was just sitting at the kitchen table, waiting for her to finish her conversation, when I saw this card for her doctor's appointment. It was there – in plain view – on top of a stack of mail.'

'So you took it.'

'Yes.'

'Without telling her, of course.'

'Naturally,' Caroline nodded, almost defiantly. 'I thought you would want to know about this.'

With his legs still stretched before him, Price rested his head against the back of the sofa and shut his eyes. 'So, Amanda is pregnant,' he said.

'You didn't know?'

'No.'

Caroline got up and went to the window but she saw none of the changing colours of the landscape before her. Turning, she looked back at Price, concern clouded her vision. 'Do you want me to go?' she asked softly.

'Yeah,' he replied. 'I need to think.'

'This is something you needed to know about, isn't it?'

He nodded.

Caroline gathered up her bag and car keys. When she

reached the door, she turned back toward him once more. 'Is...is there any chance this is not your baby?'

Price continued to sit exactly as he was. 'No,' he answered in a voice that was void of emotion. He knew the baby was his. He ran his hands over his eyes, then leaned forward, resting his elbows on his knees, his head bent. *A baby.* He breathed deeply. Responsibility hadn't just come knocking at his door, it had come crashing through, nearly knocking him off his feet.

Waiting until he heard the door close as Caroline let herself out, he stood slowly, finished buttoning his shirt, then unzipped the fly of his jeans so he could tuck his shirt in. That done, he headed toward the bedroom in search of his wallet, keys and a pair of shoes. There was little doubt as to what he would do. Unexpectedly the image of Shelley flashed across his mind. Even after all this time, it still hurt to think about her. During the drive over to Amanda's apartment, Price weighed what he had to do against his desire to keep his life uncluttered and orderly. But each time he tried to decide the best way to handle this situation, his anger kept got in the way. Dammit, not only had Amanda lied to him the night they made love, she was also planning to deceive him, to hide her pregnancy from him.

He knew where she lived. He had driven by there many times. A few times he had even got out of the car, intending to go and see her, but each time he had changed his mind. As he approached her apartment building, Price looked around at the neighbourhood. It probably looked the same today as it did fifty years ago. The apartments were old, but well maintained. The sun porches, empty now except for the covered barbecue grills and the straggling plants that remained in terracotta pots, were trimmed in white and adorned with climbing trails of ivy that clung to the building's sturdy, red brick façade. It made a charming, old-fashioned picture.

Price wondered if she would look any different to him. *Probably not*, he thought, *it's too soon. But she is different. In just a few short months, I have managed to change her life. And mine*, he added as an afterthought.

Bounding from the car, he raced up the stairway with an energy that came from wanting to get this over with as quickly as possible. No use prolonging the inevitable – it was time for a showdown. Standing in front of her door, he thought about the first time he had met her. He had waited in the car while Bobby Singleton's little sister had gone inside to get Amanda. Since both girls were too young to drive, Bobby had been charged with taking his sister and Amanda into town and dropping them off at a movie. It seemed so long ago. Now things were so much more complicated than they should be. He took a deep breath, then rang the bell.

Amanda felt better since she had taken her walk. As she climbed up the stairs to her apartment, she was startled to see a man at her door. When she reached the landing, she stopped.

Price turned. Rays of sunlight beaming through the large window in the hallway picked out all the highlights in her hair. He had the advantage of the first few seconds it took for her eyes to adjust to the light to look at her carefully. She was still Amanda – still beautiful, still desirable – only now she was pregnant with his child!

Knowing just that one piece of information had, in the span of less than an hour, forced him to reassess his life. Even though he knew he had only himself to blame, reacting to events already set in motion was not an easy task for him. Now he had to take control of a situation he neither wanted or needed.

Leaning against the door, he inquired, 'How have you been, Amanda?'

She squinted against the brightness. 'I…' She started to

answer, the surprise at seeing him evident in her voice, then she stopped. 'What do you want, Price?' she asked curtly as she pushed past him to unlock her door. The sight of him sent her emotions spinning in crazy directions.

Price followed her into the apartment and, instead of answering her, he walked on past her and peered into her studio. She had gone no farther than the doorway, leaning against its framework for support. Both hands gripped the doorknob behind her while her head rested against the hard, unyielding surface.

He turned to look at her, his hands shoved into the pockets of his jeans, his legs spread apart, his stance challenging. 'When were you planning to tell me?'

'I don't know what you're talking about,' she said, gripping the doorknob with all her strength. But she did. *My God! Was there a big 'P' for pregnant stamped on her forehead? Or maybe it was an even bigger 'S' for stupid!* She could feel the colour draining from her face and her skin grow clammy. Her heart was pounding erratically.

'Yes, you do. I'm talking about the fact that you're pregnant.' While his voice remained flat and unemotional, he was afraid his expression betrayed him, revealing the bitterness he felt at this unexpected turn his life had taken.

But what about her life? He couldn't help but notice how pale she was. Briefly, he wondered if her pallor was due to her condition or to this confrontation. And even though much of her figure was hidden under her sweater, he could tell from the hollows in her cheeks that she was definitely thinner than the last time they were together. For a moment, he felt a genuine twinge of remorse, a definite softening inside of him. This was his child Amanda was carrying. But this was not the time to let his resolve falter. She had deliberately chosen to keep it a secret from him.

How could he know? Then Amanda remembered – Caroline! She had been here only a short while ago. But there was no way she could have…the appointment card. It had been on the table. She had meant to put it away. *Oh, dear God!*

Abandoning all attempts to restrain her temper, Amanda said, 'How dare you come barging in here like this! I have nothing to say to you, Price.' She stepped away from the door, one hand still gripping the doorknob. 'Now, please leave.' Her hands were trembling, and if he didn't leave soon she was afraid her whole body would begin to shake.

Slowly, he came toward her, icy blue eyes holding hers by sheer force of will. He stopped only inches away, his expression hard and unyielding. There was no warmth around his eyes or mouth, nothing to cushion the hard edge of his voice as he commanded, 'You are going to marry me.'

His words were like a stinging slap in the face, and they jarred her into action. As the full import of what he had just said registered, Amanda stepped away from him and went toward the window. She was stunned, and right now she needed these few moments to make sense of it.

Then she spun back to face the man who had wrought such change in her life. Her conflicting emotions gave fire to her words. 'You know, Price, you're very good at using people, then discarding them. You're also used to getting your way and having your directions followed. But right now, Price McCord, you had better listen to what I have to say.'

Once more his eyes locked with hers and he saw the fury there as she advanced toward him.

'I have no idea what brought you here today. I don't know where you got your information, but you are wrong. You may be having an attack of conscience for the shabby way you treated me, or maybe it's because you duped me into believing that you cared about me. You *should* feel bad about that – so bad that you lay awake every night trying to think of ways to beg my forgiveness. But I don't want anything from you. If I had known how unprincipled you were, I would not have slept with you. I wouldn't have even sold my house to you. So you can see that, for me, the thought of marrying you for any reason – real or imagined – is ludicrous!'

'Stop it, Amanda,' Price commanded. He kept his eyes on hers as he reached into his shirt pocket and withdrew the appointment card Caroline had given him and held it out to her. 'I know,' he said.

Amanda took a step away, determined to put some space between them in spite of her suddenly weak knees. But he was quicker, grabbing her by the waist and pulling her against him. He was solid and unmoving. She arched away from him, but he responded by wrapping his arms around her. Everywhere he touched her, she felt his imprint.

'We can make this work.'

'No.'

'What about the baby, Amanda? Think about what's right,' he whispered.

From behind clenched teeth, she said, 'Let me go. I don't want anything more to do with you.' The feel and smell of him assailed her senses. The heat that she felt from his touch caused her to tremble against her will and she cursed this power he had over her.

He dropped his arms and took a step back. Then he took a deep breath and with one hand he gently tipped her fragile face upward so that she had to look at him. His eyes softened and the line of his lips relaxed. It was almost a smile. 'I want our child to have everything he or she deserves, and that includes a mother and father who are married.'

Ignoring his new tactic, Amanda answered him in the same tone he had used with her only minutes ago. 'I want you to leave me alone.'

Price's eyes hardened once more. Gone was the conciliatory tone. 'I will,' he said, 'just as soon as we're married.'

With that, he leaned down and kissed her and even though his lips were almost punishing, he still sent waves of heat and excitement pulsating through her. Then, just as quickly as it had begun, the kiss ended.

Price shook his head. 'Relax, Amanda. Once we're married you won't have anything to worry about. I'll see that you and the baby are taken care of.'

Amanda gasped. How could he be so cold and detached after the emotions he had just aroused in her? He sounded so remote, so mechanical.

'No,' she cried. 'I won't do it. There is no way you can force me to marry you.'

Price set her back away from him. Then, without touching her, he focused his laser blue eyes on hers and delivered the final blow, enunciating each word clearly, concisely and brutally. 'There is no room for discussion. I have never shirked my responsibilities and I'm not about to start now. However, you are right about one thing, honey. I cannot force you to marry me. But I can do other things.'

'You're bluffing.' She desperately hoped he was, but the look on his handsome face said otherwise.

'No, I'm not. If you don't agree to this marriage, I will sue for custody of my child immediately after it is born.'

Amanda's eyes widened in shock, her hands flew to her face as she cried out in protest.

More than anything, Price wished that he could have taken back his cruel words, but he had gone too far for that now. They had both crossed a line they shouldn't have. He had already made up his mind that he would do whatever was necessary to ensure his child's future and keep Amanda with him. Marriage was not something on his agenda. In fact, it wouldn't have appeared anywhere on his five-year plan — if he had one. But a baby changed all that. And, if he wanted to be honest, so had Amanda. But this was not the time to show weakness — at least not to a woman as stubborn as this one.

'I...I don't believe you,' she said.

In a voice that was both unemotional and controlled he continued, 'Think about it. My resources are much greater than yours. You couldn't afford a long court battle.'

'But no court in the country would give you custody,' she cried. 'You can't even prove that the baby is yours.'

'Yes, I can,' replied Price. 'And I wouldn't even have to resort to DNA testing to do it. You are incapable of lying under oath, Amanda. You would have to tell the truth in court. All I have to do is have my lawyer ask you if I'm the baby's father. Somewhere, I'll find a judge that will award me custody. It could drag on for years, but that wouldn't stop me.'

Tears welled in her eyes as Amanda realised that much of what Price said was true. She couldn't afford a long court battle, and she would never lie under oath — even about the identity of her baby's father.

'You are a monster,' she sobbed. 'I hate you!'

'It's your choice,' he said. 'You can marry me and we'll both share our baby, or you can fight me and lose everything. Which do you want?'

Oh, God. What an awful mess. This wasn't the way things were supposed to be. She bowed her head, acknowledging her defeat. 'I'll marry you,' she whispered with a heart that ached, then turned away from him. Tears gathered in her eyes then spilled over and ran down her cheeks. The joy and happiness she had always longed for had been denied her by this cold and unfeeling man.

'You'll be a father,' she said raggedly as she delivered her ultimatum, 'but you'll never be my husband.'

'Is that a threat, Amanda?'

'I'll marry you because I have no other choice, but I'll never sleep with you.'

'Never is a long time, babe. Are you sure you can live with those terms?'

chapter ten

Almost immediately, Price was filled with remorse. He had got what he came here for – Amanda was going to marry him – but it was a bittersweet victory.

This should have been a time of happiness for both of them. Instead, he had threatened her and succeeded in forcing her to agree to a marriage she didn't want. Hell, it was a marriage he didn't want either. It was, however, the right thing to do, and when backed against a wall, Price McCord always did the right thing. Shelley could attest to that.

Odd that he had found himself thinking about Shelley lately, certainly more often than he wanted, but now it was almost inevitable that she should be on his mind. Especially after the unwelcome news he had received today. But things would be different this time, he would make sure of that.

From the moment he had seen the card that Caroline had brought to him, he had known that he could no longer deny what he felt for Amanda. It was there, along with the anger and frustration at his own stupidity, and the resentment he felt at being forced to do something out of a sense of responsibility – because he had to, not because he had chosen to. But this would pass.

So he had to change his life. So what? He was thirty-two, successful, financially secure and, in a moment of absolute truth, he would have to admit that he was in love with Amanda Hamilton. It happened the day he had knocked at her door and she had answered, wearing only a blue robe and a towel on her head. It was then that he had recognised her and remembered the first time he had seen her, all skinny arms and legs, her brown eyes nearly hidden by a fringe that had grown too long.

At fifteen, she had been a waif, a shadow, shy and sweet. He had laughed at her that summer, and the antics that were no doubt inspired by Bobby's sister. But he had also seen the sadness in her eyes, when she thought no one was looking. And he wanted to tell her then that things would be OK. Now, tonight, he had seen that same look in her eyes, and he had botched the chance to erase that look, to let her know that things would work out.

All he had had to do was say he loved her. It had been his intention to tell her that, but the anger and hurt he felt toward her for not telling him about the baby overrode every other thought and emotion. And even though she had agreed to marry him, she had made it clear that she had no intention of being his wife.

Amanda didn't sleep at all that night, her mind ravaged by doubt, filled with thoughts of what she had agreed to. As she tossed and turned, she alternated between berating herself for being intimidated into marriage, and wondering how she would be able to stand being so close to Price and not letting him know how much she loved him. Even though he had been cold and unfeeling, she remembered beyond that – to the tender lover who had schooled her in the ways of love, who had showed her the way to such wanton passion that she could forget everything but that moment, who awakened such feelings of tenderness toward him.

Maybe in the light of the following day, she would conclude that this arrangement with Price was best for the baby. Maybe she could come to terms with a marriage that would be empty, reminding her each day that she was tied to a man who didn't love her, who only saw their union as a responsibility. Maybe she could handle that. *Maybe.*

Her childhood had been a solitary one in spite of the

special relationship she had shared with her grandmother. For all the love that Margaret Hamilton showered on Amanda, it was still only a substitute for the real closeness found only in a family. Amanda knew she was different, and even though she tried not to let it bother her as a child, she had always shied away from close friendships, feeling awkward when asked where her mother and father were.

Her father, Margaret's only child, had been killed in an automobile accident when Amanda was fifteen. When her mother had remarried within the year, Amanda's visit with Margaret turned into a permanent arrangement, a convenience for Susan and her new husband. Through the years there had been erratic visits, but Susan had always said she felt uncomfortable around her dead husband's mother so she never stayed long. She knew that Margaret Hamilton had disapproved of her long before she abandoned Amanda in favour of a new husband, a husband who had no intention of being encumbered by a child – his or anyone else's.

Each time her mother arrived for a visit, Amanda would wait apprehensively until she was ready to leave then Amanda would ask if she could go home with her. Each time she was disappointed when she was left behind. After a while, she stopped asking.

No, she didn't want her baby to grow up without the security of a family. Being married to Price would provide stability, and she was certain that he would love their child just as she would. Somehow, she had to make things work.

Amanda managed to make it through the next day, waiting for the phone to ring then jumping each time the shrill sound penetrated her thoughts. It wasn't until late that night that she heard from Price. When she answered the phone, she was startled that the voice at the other end could still send her blood racing. Would he always affect her this way?

He was, however, anything but endearing as he divulged the reason for his call. 'I've made all the arrangements for the wedding, Amanda. If you don't approve you had better let me know now so that I can change them. We'll be married a week from Saturday at Mike and Caroline's home.'

'A week from Saturday? That's...it's so soon.'

'Is there any reason to change it?' asked Price.

'No, I suppose not.'

'Caroline can help you shop for a dress and whatever else you need. She'll call you in the morning.'

Amanda panicked. Her funds were dangerously low in spite of the recent sale of the house. With the bank paid off and all the extra expenses of moving, there had been only a little left over for emergencies. And the cheque she was expecting from the publisher had not yet arrived.

'That's not necessary, Price,' she said quickly. 'I can shop on my own.'

Price detected a trace of panic in her voice. Hoping to ease her concern, he said, 'I've already opened accounts today at several stores for you, and I've given Caroline some idea of what you should have. The selections are up to you, of course. It will be a chance for the two of you to get to know each other.'

At first, Amanda bristled at the arrangements, then she backed down, tried to put things into perspective, and realised his gesture was meant to be both thoughtful and generous. 'I'll be glad to have Caroline come along with me, but I'll buy my own dress and anything else I need.'

The argument she expected from him was not forthcoming. Instead, he ignored her last comment. 'By the way, there will be a family dinner next Thursday evening at the Century Club. I'll pick you up at seven.'

'Uh, exactly how much family do you have besides Caroline?'

'The normal amount.'

'Do we have to go?'

'Yes, we have to go,' answered Price. 'My mother and father will be there, along with Caroline and her husband, Mike, and my Aunt Louise.' When this was greeted with silence at the other end of the phone, Price continued, 'For God's sake, Amanda, this is not an execution, it's a wedding.'

'It feels like an execution,' she mumbled. On the other end of the line, she could hear Price draw a long deep breath. Probably an exercise in self-control, she surmised, and God knows that was something he needed to work on.

'Only to you,' he said finally. 'Everyone else is expecting this to be a happy occasion so maybe you could try to act like a bride-to-be for the few hours that this dinner will take. The wedding itself will be small, only the family and a few close friends along with anyone you would like to invite. Is that satisfactory?' Price deliberately avoided any reference to her family. Sam Johnson had told him about Amanda's mother.

'Yes,' she answered with a sigh.

'Good. I'll see you Thursday evening.'

So efficient and businesslike, thought Amanda, and she was disappointed. In spite of the circumstances, she had foolishly expected things to be more romantic. As she lay in bed thinking about the arrangements Price had made, she knew her guest list would include only Sam Johnson and Joan, who would be her maid of honour.

Then, because it was late and she felt so alone, she reached for the phone and dialled her mother's number. It was three hours earlier in California. Just as she was about to hang up, the housekeeper answered.

'Millie, this is Amanda. How are you?'

'Fine, thank you.'

'Is my mother there?'

'No, Amanda, I'm sorry. Your mother and stepfather are

out of the country and won't return for another three weeks.'

'Oh. Did they leave a number where they can be reached?' she asked hopefully.

'No,' answered the housekeeper. 'They were planning to travel around, but your mother did say she would call later in the week. Can I give her a message?'

'Thanks, but I don't think...Millie? Would you please tell her that I'm getting married a week from Saturday?'

'I'll let your mother know, Amanda, and I hope you'll be very happy.'

Amanda hung up the phone disappointed. She knew she shouldn't care, but she did. She always had. Getting married was an important event. Surely her mother would want to know, even though Amanda doubted she would have come for the wedding even if she had been in the country. Maybe it was best to just get this over with and not prolong the anxiety.

Amanda wished there had been a way she could have gracefully declined the shopping expedition with Caroline. She hated Price's sister to know how much she would spend on her dress, especially since it would only be a fraction of what someone like Caroline would anticipate. But Amanda was determined that she would buy only what she could afford. It was a matter of pride, and she would be damned if she would let Price pay for her wedding dress.

Over lunch the following day, Amanda explained all this to Caroline. 'So I hope you'll understand,' concluded Amanda.

'I understand perfectly,' answered Caroline, 'but I'm not sure that Price will. He was insistent that you use the accounts he opened for you. But since it's your wedding and your money, you tell me where you'd like to start and I'll go along to give you my opinion – but only if you ask.'

Amanda smiled, already feeling better about the task ahead. 'It's a deal.'

Caroline thought that she was going to like Amanda a lot. She already liked her for her decision regarding her wedding dress. It would have been so very easy to take her brother up on his offer, and most of the women Price had dated wouldn't have hesitated to take advantage of his generosity. Shelley was a prime example of that. While they were together, she spent as much of Price's money as she could.

During the next few hours, they went from store to store looking for exactly the right dress. Finally Amanda found what she was looking for. It was an unadorned creamy white satin dress with a square neckline and gathered sleeves that tapered to stitched pleats just above the elbow. The skirt was slim, gathered at the waist and tapered toward the ankle-length hem. The styling was reminiscent of the Edwardian era. It was certainly a romantic dress, Caroline told Amanda, but privately she thought it was much too plain.

As they left the shop, Amanda asked Caroline if she had time for one more stop. When said yes, Amanda led her to a fabric store. There, in the bridal section, Amanda found the ribbon, lace and beads she needed to complete her wedding dress. Caroline eagerly joined in the selection and almost an hour later they emerged from the store, their arms loaded with packages.

On the drive home, Amanda tallied up her purchases. In addition to her wedding dress, she had bought matching satin shoes and a delicate blue silk dress to wear the night of the family dinner. At Caroline's insistence, and because she secretly wanted them, Amanda also bought a beautiful nightgown and matching robe. After all, she reasoned, she could hardly tell her future sister-in-law that she wouldn't be needing anything special for her wedding night because she would be sleeping alone.

Caroline dropped Amanda off outside her apartment building. As they parted, Amanda said, 'One of these days, I might thank you for taking that card off my kitchen table and giving it to Price. Right now, I'm not sure how I feel about it. But I do know you meant well and I hope we can be friends.'

Caroline winced at the mention of the card. 'You'll thank me, Amanda, sooner than you think. I know Price loves you and I'm glad you're going to be part of our family. I'll see you at dinner on Thursday.'

As she unlocked the door to her apartment, Amanda thought about what Caroline had said about being part of a family. That was something she hadn't thought about, but it made her feel good. She only hoped the rest of Price's family liked her as well.

That night, her thoughts turned to the wedding. How different it would be from what she had always imagined. Amanda shut her eyes. Without a church ceremony, she wouldn't get to experience any of the romantic traditions she had always dreamed about. Not even a honeymoon. In the darkness, Amanda's eyes flew wide open. *A honeymoon.* She hadn't even considered the possibility. Price hadn't mentioned anything. Surely under the circumstances he wouldn't expect…no, of course not.

There would be no honeymoon. Absolutely not.

Long before she was ready, it was time to meet Price's family. Amanda dressed carefully in the delicate blue silk dress, wanting everything to be just perfect, wanting to look just right.

Price arrived to pick her up promptly at seven. He wore a dark grey suit and, with his tanned face and his dark hair, he was more handsome than ever. It was the first time they had been face-to-face since the afternoon he had found out that she was pregnant. For a moment, they could only stare at one another.

Price spoke first. 'You look beautiful.' His voice was warm and intimate.

'Thank you,' Amanda said, dipping her head, then went to get her bag and coat. He took her coat from her arms and held it for her.

Slipping her arms into the sleeves, Amanda moved to step away from him, but he was quicker and he stalled her with his hands on her shoulders. He held her that way for only a moment, but for Amanda it was long enough. Then, without speaking, Price released her and turned to hold the door open.

For most of the drive, their conversation was about the wedding preparations. Then, unable to stand the strain any longer, she asked the question she could no longer put off. 'Price, does your family know about me?'

'What about you?' he asked softly, his eyes seeking hers in the darkness.

'Well, that you're marrying me because...'

'They know that I'm marrying you, nothing more,' he said sharply, cutting her off in mid-sentence. 'Come on, Amanda, this is supposed to be a happy occasion.'

'But aren't they going to wonder why all this is happening so quickly?'

'It's the way I do things. They may wonder, but it won't surprise any of them. Actually, they are really very happy that I'm getting married. My family is going to love you. Quit worrying and try to act as though you're happy,' Price said lightly as he turned into the driveway that led to the country club.

'There's something else,' she said. 'I was wrong about you and your plans for the house, wasn't I?'

He nodded.

'In the beginning, did you consider using the house for a development?'

'I considered it, then I dismissed it. The site wasn't right. It's too isolated. Besides, I wanted the house for myself. It is a truly beautiful place, Amanda. One of these days, we'll be living there together.'

'I'm sorry that I jumped to conclusions. I just wanted to tell you that before we go in to meet your parents.'

'A confession, huh?' Price asked teasingly. 'I understand it's good for the soul.'

'It is,' Amanda replied, smiling. 'You should try it sometime.'

Price sobered and a troubled look crossed his face. 'I will,' he said. 'Now let's go in.'

He came around the car and held the door for her, then as he led her up the stairs to meet his waiting parents, he knew he would have to tell Amanda about Shelley soon. He was running out of time. And excuses.

The club was old and prestigious, the entry impressive with crystal chandeliers that hung suspended from an ornate and intricately embellished plaster ceiling. Hundreds of crystal prisms glittered and were reflected in the mirror finish of the marble floor.

Kate McCord looked around anxiously, unable to follow the conversation between her husband, Ed, and his sister, Louise. What kind of woman was Price marrying, she wondered. She had never cared for any of the women he had dated. And Shelley, well, she had been such a disappointment. Now she wondered if Price had really considered what a change this marriage would mean to him.

Kate spotted her handsome son immediately and, breaking away from the rest of the family, she quickly made her way toward her only son and his bride-to-be.

As she surveyed her surroundings, Amanda saw a petite woman with auburn hair the colour of Caroline's bearing down upon them and knew this had to be Price's mother. She turned toward Price and, just as she was about speak, his hand circled her arm to steer her across the lobby.

'Relax,' he instructed. 'Here comes my mother.'

The small woman was a bundle of energy, and the smile that lit her face was both welcoming and genuine. Amanda felt herself smiling in return. Within seconds, Price had one arm around his mother and the other around Amanda. Excitedly, Kate guided Price and Amanda toward the rest of the family.

Price's father, Ed, had the same lazy smile as his son and Price watched with pride as his family put Amanda completely at ease. It was obvious that they all approved of what they saw.

Once they were seated in the dining room, the waiter brought champagne to the table and, when it had been served, Ed McCord tapped lightly on his glass to get everyone's attention. 'A toast,' he announced jovially, 'to the beautiful bride and the lucky groom.' Then he continued in a more serious vein. 'We are very pleased to welcome you to our family, Amanda.'

To the ring of crystal filled with the sparkling amber wine, Amanda blinked back an unexpected rush of tears. Noticing how moved she was by his father's words, Price reached for her hand and squeezed it reassuringly.

Louise, Price's aunt, was the quietest of the group. During dinner she leaned over to Price and whispered, 'These gatherings always focus on the bride-to-be. What about the groom? Is he happy to throw aside the carefree life of a bachelor?'

Price smiled and shook his head ruefully. 'To tell you the truth, Louise, I don't know. Ask me again in six months.'

Louise nodded, not in agreement, but in understanding. She had long held that all men entered into marriage reluctantly, sometimes only as a last resort to get what they wanted.

'Have you told Amanda about Shelley?' she whispered.

'No,' answered Price.

'Don't wait, Price. She has a right to know. Don't start your marriage off with secrets, especially one that important.'

chapter eleven

'I really like your family,' Amanda said on the ride home. 'They made me feel so welcome. It was wonderful.'

Price looked over at her as they drove toward her apartment. 'I guess it's something you take for granted until someone reminds you how special your family really is.'

All evening, Amanda had studied him as he interacted with his parents, seeing a side of him she had never glimpsed before. They mattered to him. She was sure that his child would play a big part in his life, but what kind of part would she play? She knew that Price resented her announcement that she had no intention of having sex with him, but did he know that these terms were going to be just as difficult for her?

Amanda's mood became sombre as she dared to voice a question that had been nagging at her. 'Price, will your family still be as happy for you when they find out that this marriage is something you felt you had to do? You would have never wanted to marry me if you hadn't found out I was pregnant.'

He turned his attention away from the road and she could feel his probing eyes on her. 'Are you sure?' he asked in a slow, husky voice. Startled, she raised her eyes to meet his. His expression was unreadable, his face hidden in shadow. Her throat suddenly went dry as she recalled the night they had first made love. It was more painful now that she knew she couldn't escape him.

'You made that very clear, Price. Right from the beginning, or more accurately, right after we made love. You let me know that you wanted nothing more to do with me because I was the kind who would expect a man to love her and to marry her. You didn't want that then – and you still don't.'

'Fate has played a dirty trick on both of us,' continued Amanda. 'I used to dream about marrying a man who would love me. Instead, I'm having a baby and the only reason I'm going to be married is because the man responsible wants to be a father. He has also threatened to sue for custody if I don't agree to marry him. This is not exactly the basis for a happy marriage, is it?'

'Is that why you insist on marriage without sex, Amanda? Because you think that none of this would have happened if I hadn't been careless and you hadn't got pregnant?' asked Price.

She avoided his question. 'It wasn't your fault. I'm no child. I should have thought about taking precautions but I didn't think that we…that I…I, uh, lied when you asked me about it. I was too embarrassed to admit that not only hadn't I done this before, I also didn't have any plans to do it any time soon.'

Price paused then restated his question, his voice sharp and cutting. 'I want an answer. Why are you insisting that sex should not be a part of this marriage?'

'Because I know why you want to marry me,' she answered. 'You want this baby and I just happen to be part of the deal. Well, sex isn't going to be one of the fringe benefits. I can't make love to a man who can't love me back.'

He pulled up in front of her apartment building and switched off the ignition. When he had helped her out of the car and shut the door, he nudged her back against the car, pressing his thighs against her, making his arousal evident as he leaned into her and took advantage of her surprise.

Amanda hadn't expected this and the heat of him pressing against her sent a fire racing through her. She fought the almost overwhelming urge to answer the sensual messages his body was telegraphing to hers. Her mind raced. If she couldn't resist him now, what was she going to do when they were sharing the same house? How would she be able to control her desire for him?

Price leaned forward, his arms and hands trapping her completely while his lips met hers in a hard, demanding kiss that wiped all thought from her mind. She helplessly answered his demands. When his lips left hers and travelled to the soft hollow at the base of her throat, she felt lost. With practised hands, Price swiftly unbuttoned the front of her dress, the pale blue silk rustling lightly in protest as he slowly pushed it down to bare her shoulders and the soft swell of her breasts.

Amanda's head was thrown back against the hard, unyielding metal body of the car. Her most primitive instincts kicked in as Price's mouth returned to hers, this time barely touching or caressing, but teasing instead.

'See how easy it is, honey?' he whispered as he drew away from her, delighting in her flushed appearance, her tousled hair, her moist, parted lips. Her eyes were glazed, her breath quick and shallow. It took her long seconds to understand what had happened. 'Passion is easy,' Price said, his voice laced with amusement. 'Another few minutes and you would be completely out of that dress, begging me to make love to you. I don't want a marriage without sex and neither do you.'

Realising how foolish he had made her appear, Amanda felt only humiliation as she pushed away from him and started for the door. When she reached the top step, she turned. Price was leaning against the car where she had left him, his hands in his pockets, his feet crossed at the ankles. His face reflected the amusement and satisfaction he felt at having made his point.

Taking in his stance and his obviously amused expression, Amanda felt anger surge through her. *He was laughing at her!* Without thinking, she ran down the steps to confront him. How dare he play with her emotions like that?

'I'll never forgive you for this.' Her voice was low and shaky as she raised her hand to slap him. But he reached out and easily grabbed her wrist, holding it rigidly in mid-air.

With his face only scant inches away, his breath mingled with hers. 'Don't start something with me that you can't finish. One way or another, I'll have you in my bed, Amanda, and I'll make love to you in ways you've never even dreamed about. You may think you hate me, but I just proved that I can arouse you to the point where you stop thinking about everything – except what I can make you feel.'

Suddenly, Price released her wrist and stepped away from her. He went around to the other side of the car then turned and looked over at her.

She hadn't moved. Her eyes were wide with disbelief, her face flushed with anger.

'I'll have you whenever I want you. Count on it, babe.'

When Amanda awakened the next morning, she was troubled. Last night with Price had been emotionally draining. Slowly she got up and made her way to the kitchen. She had lost control of her life. Today was Friday. Tomorrow she was getting married. How could she go through with this?

The phone rang and she ran to answer it.

'Amanda, good morning. This is Kate. I didn't wake you, did I?'

'No,' Amanda replied. 'I was just having coffee. How are you?'

'Fine. I was going to invite you out to lunch today, Amanda, but then I realised that you must have a lot of last minute things to do before the wedding. May I come over and see you instead?'

'Why, yes,' answered Amanda, surprised and pleased at the request. 'I'd love to see you.'

'I'll be there at noon,' said Kate, 'and I'll bring lunch for us.'

Amanda hung up and sat down with a sigh. When had her life got so complicated? She was about to marry into a family she could easily love, but she was going to have a husband who didn't want her. What a mess. Looking around the kitchen idly, Amanda speculated what her life would be like with Price.

What do you say over coffee in the morning to a man who married you only because you were pregnant? Rubbing the back of her hand over her eyes, she wished that tomorrow was over with. Shouldn't a bride look forward to her wedding day? She had never imagined that things would turn out this way, but then why not? Nothing else in her life had turned out the way she had wanted!

Late into the previous night, Kate and Ed McCord had discussed the wedding. Not only did they approve of Price's bride-to-be, they were immensely surprised at his choice. For one thing, Amanda was younger than they had expected, and vastly different from the women Price usually dated. Together they made a striking couple. But even though Price had been charming and attentive toward Amanda all evening, Kate had sensed that something was not quite right between them. Price had told them that the girl had no family, and because of this Kate felt drawn to her. Her son was too old to need a mother, but maybe Amanda needed a friend to talk to.

Kate knocked at the door of Amanda's apartment promptly at noon. Amanda glanced around the apartment once more before opening the door to her soon-to-be mother-in-law. Everything was neat and shining.

She wasn't nervous about seeing Kate, but she was apprehensive about discussing the wedding. What if Kate found out that this wasn't exactly a marriage made in heaven?

Later, after the two women had finished lunch, Amanda cleared the table and served coffee. When she was once again seated, Kate reached into her bag and brought out a small box which she handed to Amanda. 'I've brought you something. It's my wedding gift to my new daughter-in-law. They belonged to Price's grandmother and I was hoping you might wear them on your wedding day.'

Amanda's eyes widened in surprise. She hadn't expected this. 'But what about Caroline? Surely you would want your daughter to have these?'

'No,' said Kate. 'When Caroline married, I gave her other jewellery that also belonged to her grandmother. She will keep it for her children, just as I hope you keep these and pass them down when you and Price have a family.'

Slowly, Amanda took the box from Kate, her fingers shaking as she opened it. Inside was a pair of delicate pearl earrings mounted in gold with a small cluster of diamonds nestled next to the pearl. They were exquisite.

Amanda looked up at Kate her eyes filling with tears. 'I...thank you,' she said. 'They are beautiful. I've never had anything like this before.' Amanda looked up from the earrings and her eyes met Kate's. 'I'll always cherish them. My grandmother never cared for jewellery and for that reason she never owned anything other than her gold wedding band. I guess you could say that she was a no-nonsense kind of woman.'

'The best kind,' murmured Kate as she looked at this lovely girl, so moved by her gift. Her heart went out to her and she reached over and hugged Amanda quickly. 'Welcome to our family. We're very happy that Price has chosen to marry you.'

Amanda looked at Kate through misty eyes and

suddenly she buried her face in her hands and began to cry in earnest.

Kate was concerned. 'Oh, Amanda! I'm sorry. What have I done? Was it something I said?'

'Nothing,' sobbed Amanda. 'You are so kind and I don't deserve it.'

'Why not?' asked Kate softly.

'Because you brought me this wonderful gift, because you think this marriage is just wonderful, and because you think Price and I are so happy.' Amanda cried even harder.

Kate's face mirrored her concern. She reached for Amanda's hand and said, 'It's just wedding jitters, honey. You have every right to cry, but by tomorrow everything will be fine.'

Amanda shook her head to signal her disagreement, sniffling and reaching for a tissue. Dabbing at her eyes she said, 'Price doesn't love me.'

'Of course he does,' said Kate softly.

'No, he doesn't.'

After a pause Kate said, 'But you love him, don't you?'

Amanda looked up through reddened eyes and said candidly, 'I've loved him since the moment I saw him, only I never thought he would be attracted to me.'

Kate patted Amanda's hand reassuringly. 'Price is marrying you so he must love you. It was obvious to all of us at dinner last night that he can't keep his eyes off you. He's very much in love, Amanda. I've never seen him this way around another woman.' *Not even Shelley*, added Kate silently.

Amanda looked up quickly in surprise. Kate smiled back reassuringly. 'The spark is definitely there. Price may have a difficult time telling you what he feels, but believe me, he would never propose marriage if he didn't love you.'

'Oh, Kate,' sighed Amanda. 'This is so awful. Price didn't propose. He's forcing me to marry him.'

This time, it was Kate who registered surprise. 'Forcing you? But that can't be true. No one can force you to marry.'

'Price can, and he is. And the terrible thing is that even though I hate him for it, I still want to marry him,' Amanda sniffed. 'I love him, but he doesn't love me.' She looked at Kate and saw the confusion on her face. 'This doesn't make any sense to you, does it? I should have never mentioned this to you, Kate. I'm so sorry. It's not fair for me to burden you with my problems, especially when they concern Price.'

'That's not so, Amanda. I asked to see you today so that I could…well, let you know that since your mother is not around, I could fill that role if you want. And it looks very much like you do need someone. Now, do you want to tell me all about you and Price from the beginning?'

Amanda nodded. 'He has turned my life upside down. I've never been in love before. I just never met the right person, but since I saw Price again I've certainly made up for lost time. He made it very clear to me from the beginning, well almost from the beginning,' she amended, 'that he didn't want to get involved with me.' At Kate's questioning look, Amanda explained. 'Instinctively, Price knew that I would not want anything less than marriage once I had found the right man. I never told him this, he just sensed it – and he was right. He's just the opposite. He never wanted to make any kind of commitment. I should have known better. After all, he's thirty-two and single. That right there should have been a warning to me.'

'People in love don't heed warnings, Amanda,' Kate interjected softly.

'Everything that happened between us was an accident,' sighed Amanda. 'I love Price, but I knew there was no future with him, and now – now I'm pregnant.' Amanda held her breath waiting for Kate to say something, to judge her, to condemn and pass sentence on her, but nothing but kindness and concern crossed the older woman's face. Amanda continued. 'I never told Price. He found out quite by accident. I knew he would hate me if I forced him into a relationship he didn't want and my pride kept me from telling him. What I hadn't counted on was a visit from Caroline.'

Kate raised her brows. 'Caroline?'

'Yes,' answered Amanda. 'Caroline saw a card from my obstetrician reminding me of my next appointment…'

'…and she told Price,' concluded Kate.

Amanda nodded again. 'A week ago, Price confronted me about the baby and said that we were going to be married. He didn't ask me, he just assumed that I would do anything he wanted. When I refused, he threatened to sue me for custody of the baby once it was born, so I agreed to marry him. Kate, I don't know how I can go through with this. How can I marry a man who doesn't love me?'

Kate leaned back in her chair. It was clear that every word that Amanda spoke was the truth. Kate could not imagine Amanda deliberately setting out to entrap Price by becoming pregnant. She also knew her son. He could appear to be hard and ruthless when it suited his purposes. But she also knew he never allowed himself to be caught up in any situation unless he wanted to be.

Reflecting on Price's behaviour last night at dinner, it was clear that he was in love with Amanda. But why hadn't he told her that he loved her? Kate had almost given up hope that Price would get married. Now she suspected that Amanda had taken him by surprise, and he couldn't even admit to himself that he loved her.

Kate chose her words carefully, knowing how important they would be to Amanda. 'I'm going to give you some advice and I only hope for your sake and Price's that I'm right. I had nearly given up all hope that Price would marry. And now that he is, I'm happy. But I'm also concerned because of the circumstances.'

Amanda's eyes widened and her face turned red as she misunderstood what Kate meant. 'You mean because I'm pregnant.'

'No,' said Kate quickly as she shook her head. 'I mean that I am concerned because Price has chosen to intimidate you rather than admit he's in love with you. I think you should go ahead with the wedding. If my son has conjured up these threats, he must really want to marry you. It will be up to you to make him admit to that, Amanda, and don't you dare make things easy for him.'

Amanda smiled, and her face glowed as she reached out to grasp Kate's hand. 'I wasn't planning on it.'

Later that night in bed, Kate remembered something from her conversation with Amanda that had been nagging at her. She mentioned it to Ed as she reached to turn out the lamp. 'It wasn't what she said, it was what she didn't say. I don't think Price has told her about Shelley. I'm worried. Surely he wouldn't try to hide something like that.'

'Price is an adult, honey,' replied Ed. 'He's always exercised good judgement in the past and I'm sure he will now.'

'This is different, Ed. She's in love with him.' Kate chewed on her lip as she contemplated telling what she had learned this afternoon. 'I'm not sure that Price has exercised any judgement at all. Amanda is pregnant.'

'Pregnant?' repeated Ed, astounded. 'Dammit. Price is no kid, he's thirty-two-years-old. Doesn't he know how to keep his trousers zipped up? What the hell is wrong with him?'

'He's in love,' said Kate, 'and she loves him. That's why I'm concerned that he hasn't told her everything. I want you to talk to him, Ed.'

'About what? How to keep his...'

'Ed.'

'We had that talk a long, long time ago, Katie.'

'I'm not talking about that. I'm talking about Shelley. He has to tell her about Shelley. He can't hide the past. What on earth is wrong with him, anyway?'

Ed yawned. 'I don't know, Katie, but he gets it from your side of the family. My side of the family can't keep anything a secret for more than five minutes. Besides, they would rather just tell lies. Now can we get some sleep?'

'What if he decides not to tell her?'

Ed leaned over and kissed his wife goodnight. 'Then, Katie, my love, it's sure to come back and bite him on the ass.'

chapter twelve

Amanda began her wedding day with a feeling of apprehension and excitement, with dread and anticipation, wishing she could stop the hands of the clock, wishing that time wouldn't pass so slowly. When she imagined herself at Price's side, she became daring and dangerous. How adventurous she was to even show up for this wedding! When she imagined what would follow the marriage ceremony, she became scared and vulnerable. Only fools rush in where they're not wanted.

As soon as she had agreed to marry Price, Amanda had immediately told Joan about the wedding, but not about the circumstances that made it such a hasty affair. She explained the rush by saying it was what he wanted. For that she felt a little guilty, but her pride wouldn't let her reveal the real reason. If Joan figured it out, she had kept it to herself. Several times Amanda came close to telling her friend that she was pregnant, but something always stopped her. There would be plenty of time for that later. It was still too personal, too private, too new.

Joan arrived the apartment at ten that morning to help her get ready. 'Nervous?' she asked.

'Sick,' said Amanda, who had had a bout with morning sickness only a few hours earlier.

'It's natural for the bride to feel this way.'

Amanda managed a weak smile. *That's what you think.*

They spent the next two hours pressing their dresses and deciding on a hairstyle for Amanda. It was a way to combat nervousness. Then Joan helped Amanda pack the clothes she would be taking on her honeymoon.

'Where are you going?' Joan asked.

'I don't know,' answered Amanda. 'It's a surprise.'

And it was. Price had called her the night before and told her to pack enough clothes for a week, mostly casual, but also a few things to wear out to dinner. Amanda had been completely speechless. She had never even considered that he would want to take time off for a honeymoon. Under the circumstances, she found it highly unsettling and told him so. He had replied that he had every intention of making this a very traditional marriage. It seemed to Amanda's already taut nerves that he stressed the word 'traditional'.

By noon, Amanda was a mental mess. If Joan remarked once more on how romantic she thought this whirlwind courtship was, she would scream. Her thoughts were on Price. What was he doing now? Was he having regrets about the deal they had made?

At twelve-thirty, the limousine Price had arranged arrived to pick them up and take them to Mike and Caroline's house. As they pulled away from the curb, Amanda turned to look back at her apartment. Every day, she had become more comfortable in her new home, and she had discovered that she liked the feeling of being part of a neighbourhood. Now she was leaving that behind. In a few hours, she would be married. As Price's wife, she should be able to reasonably expect to be secure and protected, yet her future seemed more uncertain than ever.

Mike and Caroline Sloan lived in an older section of Atlanta where the homes were mansion-sized but the beautiful landscaped grounds were small by comparison. Hearing the limousine pull into the circular drive, Caroline opened the front door and hurried out to meet Amanda and Joan. After Amanda had introduced her best friend to her soon-to-be sister-in-law, Caroline showed them upstairs to a guest bedroom.

'We can hang your dresses in here,' Caroline said, opening a set of double wardrobe doors.

Impulsively, Amanda turned to Caroline and asked, 'Would you like to see my dress? I know you were terribly worried about it because it was so plain.'

Caroline blushed. 'I would love to see it.'

Unzipping the long garment bag, Amanda removed the dress.

'Oh, Amanda,' sighed Caroline, as Amanda twirled the dress around from front to back. 'I can't believe it's the same dress. It's beautiful.'

Amanda had overlaid each of the tapered sleeves and the bodice with spun cobwebs of lace, and to the lace she had then painstakingly sewn tiny sequins and pearls wherever the pattern formed a delicate flower. That same lace was repeated in a deep band just along the hem of the ankle length skirt. The overall effect was delicate and perfectly suited to Amanda. Her veil was a frothy concoction banded by the same lace as the dress.

When Caroline left them to go downstairs and check on the caterer, Amanda carefully hung the dress back in the wardrobe. Hoping for a few minutes to rest, she made her way to the bed. She had just plumped the pillows behind her back when there was knock at the door. Sitting up, she was relieved to see that it was Kate who peeked around the door.

Stepping into the room, Kate greeted Joan warmly when Amanda introduced them. Then she joined Amanda on the side of the bed. Taking both her hands, Kate whispered, 'Just remember everything I told you. Price is doing this because of you.' A look of understanding passed from the younger woman to the older and Amanda gently squeezed the hands that were holding hers.

When Kate had left the room, Joan asked, 'What was that about?'

'Just some words of wisdom from the mother of the

groom,' answered Amanda as she once again leaned back against the pillows and closed her eyes.

Joan dressed first in a tea length crepe dress in pale yellow. Then it was Amanda's turn. She could no longer put off the inevitable. When it was time to slip the dress over her head, her hands were shaking.

Joan smiled at her friend as she fastened the tiny buttons that ran up the back of the dress. 'I don't think I have ever seen you look so beautiful.' Looking at her reflection in the full-length mirror, Amanda had to agree. Her dark hair was pulled away from her face with shining curls cascading from her crown. As she put on her veil, she knew that everything was perfect. Now she only had to watch for Price's response.

From downstairs, she could hear soft music from a piano, a violin, and a cello. The scents of carefully chosen flowers drifted throughout the house. And as she took the bouquet of delicate ivory roses with their dark green leaves from Joan's outstretched hand, she noticed how the bouquet trembled. It took a moment for her to realise that it was her hands that trembled, not the flowers. Amanda shut her eyes and took a deep breath. *Now*, she thought, *it is time*.

Later, she would never be able to remember those first few seconds when she slowly descended the staircase. She was halfway down before she came into Price's view, and it was precisely at that moment that their eyes met.

Price drew his breath in sharply. His heartbeat was almost painful. His eyes turned a dark stormy blue. *My God, she's beautiful*, he thought. *In a few minutes she will be my wife, and I will have promised to love and care for her. But she doesn't want this marriage, and I know I'll never be able to keep my hands off of her.*

With each step, Amanda drew closer and the tension between them heightened. She dreaded what was to come, yet she was also strangely excited by it. She lowered her eyes, seeking release from his hypnotic gaze. Even at this distance, his blatant masculinity beckoned to her. His tall, powerful presence was enhanced by the stark contrast of the black of his tuxedo against the snowy whiteness of his shirt.

Steadily, his dark blue eyes continued to watch her approach; silently they commanded her to look at him. And when she did, the electric current that passed between them became a physical bond neither could break. As she drew even with him, he held out his hand to her. Placing her hand in his, she knew she belonged with him. She had been waiting a lifetime for this moment.

Price's gaze moved from Amanda's face to the small hand that even now trembled in his, and he was suddenly overwhelmed by a fierce desire to cherish and protect her. The intensity of it shocked him.

As if in a dream, they each repeated the vows that would bind them to one another. For that moment, there was no one else in their universe, no measure of time. They were suspended, pledging to cherish, promising to love for a lifetime.

Amanda looked at Price wordlessly, asking for his reassurance, and she found it there in his eyes, and felt it in the warmth of his smile as he leaned forward and kissed her.

Then it was over. Before she could even say a single word to him, they were surrounded by guests applauding and offering their congratulations. It occurred to Amanda as she accepted hugs and compliments, that the most difficult part of the day was still ahead. There were more people who had been invited than she had expected, and she didn't know anyone except Joan, Sam, and her new family.

Joan, sensing Amanda's momentary panic, hugged her. 'You'll be OK, Amanda. I'm so happy for you.'

To her friend, who had seen her through so many bad times, Amanda whispered her thanks.

Joan stayed close by while Amanda looked around for Price. He was only a few feet away, trying to make his way back to her. Each time she glanced at him, she found his eyes on her. It was both disconcerting and reassuring.

Turning to answer a question from a guest, she noticed a tall, stunning blonde in the lobby. Her hair was pulled into a sleek twist which accentuated her cheekbones and her green eyes. Amanda didn't remember seeing her earlier, but then there were so many new faces, each with their own ties to Price's family. Instinctively, Amanda looked past her new in-laws toward Price. He was standing with his arm draped casually over his aunt's shoulder.

Amanda knew the exact moment he caught sight of the blonde. A bitter expression passed briefly over his face and then it was gone. Hurriedly, he excused himself from the group that had formed around him, and walked across the living room toward the woman.

As she watched him go, Amanda felt a wave of jealousy. Just as Price reached the woman, she stepped forward, put her arms around his neck and kissed him. To Amanda's eyes, it was anything but congratulatory. Full blown, with sensual overtones, it was a kiss that spoke of long and easy familiarity.

Feeling a hand on her arm, Amanda turned.

'Amanda, there's someone I'd like you to meet,' Kate said. 'This is Ginny Young. Ginny and I are old friends...'

When the woman drew back, her expression was smug, satisfied.

Price's expression was guarded as he reached out to place his hands on her upper arms. With a firm grip, he set her back away from him. He was the first to speak, his face void of emotion, his brow raised questioningly. 'Is this your way of congratulating the groom?'

'It's my way of reminding the groom,' she replied archly, 'of what he's missing.'

'Cut it out, Shelley,' Price replied tersely. 'Things have been over between us for a long time. Who invited you here?'

Shelley laughed and it rang with bitterness. 'Do you honestly think that any of your family would welcome me here – for any reason? I crashed the party, Price. I heard you were getting married, and I just had to see it for myself.'

'I suggest you leave now, Shelley, before you make a bigger fool of yourself than you already have.'

Price fervently hoped that Amanda had not witnessed what had just taken place. It would require an explanation he was not ready to give. It had taken him a long time to recover from Shelley, a long and painful time. He didn't want any questions about that part of his life. Not today, not tonight.

'Aren't you going to introduce me to your bride? Maybe I can give her a few tips about what makes you happy.' said Shelley as she peered past Price's shoulder, searching for Amanda.

'Drop it, Shelley. It's time for you to leave.' Price took her arm and firmly propelled her toward the front door.

Across the room, Amanda had been too far away to overhear the conversation between Price and the woman, but there was no way she could have mistaken the kiss she had witnessed, or the fact that Price was now heading toward the front door with her.

Aware of Shelley's presence and sensing Amanda's distress, Mike, with Caroline in tow, joined Amanda and tried to distract her. But Amanda was intent on discovering what had just taken place. 'Who was the woman talking to Price a few minutes ago?' Mike looked nervously toward the front door and wished his brother-in-law would get the hell in here, where he belonged.

'That was Shelley Van Gordon. She, uh...' began Caroline, then she stopped, not certain of how to proceed. 'From a long time ago.

'An old acquaintance from Price's bachelor days,' Mike said. He flashed Caroline a warning glance, but either she didn't see him or she chose to ignore him.

'Actually,' said Caroline, her voice already fuzzy from champagne, 'there was more...' She was stopped mid-sentence by a poke in the ribs from Mike's elbow. Realising what she had almost done, she began to apologise profusely.

'It's OK, Caroline,' replied Amanda. 'Price was a bachelor a long time before I met him. I'm sure there are many women in his past.'

'Oh, yes there were. Indeed there were. But Shelley was differ...ow!' Again Caroline was stopped from revealing even more by Mike's elbow.

'I have to take Caroline away now, Amanda. Either that or she will be black-and-blue in the morning. All you have to do is give her a few glasses of champagne and she'll tell you anything, whether it's true or not, and it's almost always not.' He grinned and wrapped his arm around Caroline. 'It's an Irish thing. Give 'em a few drinks and they start telling stories.' Turning back toward Amanda, Mike said, 'I'll bring you another glass of champagne.'

'Yes, thanks, Mike. I think I need it.' Once again, Amanda scanned the room, hoping to locate Price. There were so many people. More than a few minutes ago? And it seemed so warm in here. If she could just get some air. Was Price still with the blonde?

Within minutes, Amanda saw him moving surely toward her. When he reached her side, he took her hand and she immediately felt better. Price made no mention of the woman, and all through the dinner that followed, he showered Amanda with his full attention, just as a newly married man was expected to do.

Hours later, after the newlyweds had changed into travelling clothes, they said their farewells to both family and friends, and departed in a shower of rice.

It was dark outside as they sped down the motorway. Amanda nervously bit her lip. Other than a few brief spurts of conversation, mostly about the reception, she and Price had both been quiet since they had left Caroline's. But there was one topic that had been on her mind most of the evening.

'That woman in the hallway, the tall blonde?' Amanda said.

'Uh, huh.'

Amanda waited for Price to explain, but nothing was forthcoming.

'I think Caroline said her name was Shelley Van-some-thing-or-other.

'Yeah.'

She scrunched her lips and waited or him to say more. Either Price didn't want to talk about this, or the whole exchange she had witnessed, kiss and all, didn't mean anything. *So which was it?* 'Well? Aren't you going to tell me about her?'

'I suppose that means you saw her kiss me,' Price said.

'How could I miss it?'

'Well, I could always hope. But, that's Shelley. She always did take things to the extreme.'

'I suppose that means that you know her well?'

'As well as I ever wanted to. Forget about her, honey. She hasn't been around for a long time, and what she did today was all for attention. She didn't belong there – she wasn't invited, and I got rid of her as soon as I could.'

'Oh.'

'We talked about this, remember – my past? You said you didn't want the details, right?'

'Right,' Amanda said, unaware that Price had just sidestepped a subject that not only weighed heavily on his mind, but one which he would soon have to revisit.

Reflecting on her own trepidation in the silence that followed, Amanda wondered if he was uneasy now that he was legally tied to her, or was he simply taking this marriage in stride, viewing it as yet another responsibility.

Just as she was about to say something, anything, Price took his eyes off the road and looked at her. 'Nervous?'

Amanda exhaled, unaware that she had been holding her breath. 'I suppose so. After all, it isn't every day that I get married. What about you?' she asked, then instantly wished she hadn't.

'Not at all,' Price replied. 'I'm anticipating the honeymoon. Actually, I can hardly wait.'

Amanda looked at him trying to decide if he was teasing or serious. Then she decided he was dead serious. 'Well, you had better start working on the virtue of patience,' she said, hoping he didn't detect the quiver in her voice. 'I don't think your expectations are at all realistic.'

He didn't respond. Instead he kept his eyes on the road, his mouth set in a grim line. But both of them knew the challenge that awaited them. Here they were begining a honeymoon and the bride had no intention of going to bed with her groom on their wedding night, while the groom had all his energy focused on doing just that.

It seemed that they had been driving for hours. Looking out the window, Amanda could see nothing. Unable to disperse her growing nervousness, she asked, 'Where are we? We left Caroline's over two hours ago.'

Once again, Price looked across the dark interior of the car. 'On our way to begin our honeymoon, Amanda.' His voice was low and tinged with wry humour.

'Price, tell me where we are. This is no time to be funny.'

'I didn't mean to be funny. Honeymoons are a time for couples to get to know each other without interference.'

'Dammit, I know what a honeymoon is. What I don't know is where we are.'

'Relax, honey. We're on our way to a little place called Willow Beach, about ten miles the other side of Savannah. We should get there about nine. Since we'll be staying for a week, we'll have a chance to be alone and work some things out.'

Amanda moaned in frustration. She knew exactly what he had planned for that week. The only thing he planned to 'work out' was how and when they would make love.

'I thought we should at least start off our marriage like everyone else,' he added, his expression thoughtful as he looked toward Amanda.

'This is crazy,' cried Amanda. 'And you are crazy for thinking you can do this. I don't want to spend a week alone with you. I want to get my life back to normal as quickly as possible.' She took a deep breath.

There was a long pause before Price spoke again. 'Your life will never be the same again, Amanda.' His voice was low, controlled. 'You are married to me now, and you're having my baby.'

Sobered by that thought, Amanda wisely refrained from any reply. What had she ever done to deserve this? The thought of being alone with him for even a night unnerved her. How long would it take him to wear down the pitiful amount of will power she had?

Amanda knew women who had done things far worse than she had, and they had never got caught. She had waited a long time for the right man, and two rolls-in-the-hay later she was pregnant. *What was she going to do now?* As each mile brought her closer to the beginning of her life with Price, she still had no answers.

Price had carefully planned this honeymoon. He needed time alone with her. He wanted to make love to her, to tell her he had married her because he loved her. Even with all his experience, nothing had prepared him for this night. The time had come to tell her what was in his heart.

chapter thirteen

There was no moon to break the darkness. Only the sound of waves crashing against the sand and then rushing out, slashed the silence that surrounded them. Using a torch to find his way, Price opened the front door of the seaside cottage and reached inside to flip on a light. When Amanda followed him, he stopped her before she could actually take a step inside.

'I believe it's customary for the groom to carry the bride over the threshold,' he said in a low voice as he bent down and lifted her into his arms.

Amanda smiled in defeat. She had no choice but to wrap her arms around his neck.

Once they were inside, he placed a tender kiss on her lips. 'Welcome to our honeymoon retreat, Mrs McCord,' he whispered, as he let her slide slowly from his arms, her body touching his entire length before her feet touched the floor. He held her like that for a moment longer, then released her and went outside to get their luggage.

Amanda stood where Price had left her, wishing the warmth of him was still pressed close to her. How was she going to get through this night? How could she resist a man who seemed hell-bent on making this the most exciting, romantic night of her life? She wanted to savour everything – each word, each look, each touch – but she couldn't lose sight of the real reason he had married her. *Just keep your feet on the floor*, she reminded herself, *and your head out of the clouds*.

Looking around, Amanda saw that this was a beautiful house. With one side of the living room anchored by a large stone fireplace, the room was warm and inviting.

The wall opposite the fireplace was made up of a bank of French doors that led to a brick terrace. She was sure that in the daylight she would be able to see the ocean from there.

There was no formal dining room, only a large comfortable table with six chairs that occupied a space near the kitchen. It, too, would provide a view of the beach. The kitchen was galley-style, narrow but efficient. Farther down the hallway was a bathroom. Beyond that she found a cosy nook of a room with floor-to-ceiling bookshelves that was obviously intended to be a study or office, and a spacious bedroom with an adjoining bath.

Somewhere in the numbed recesses of her mind, Amanda noted that there was only one bedroom in the house. She shivered involuntarily as she sat down on the edge of the bed, thinking of the hours ahead.

It was a romantic room with an elaborate white iron bed set in the centre of the floor. A white wicker bench sat at the foot of the bed and an antique table and two chairs occupied a space near the French doors. Outside, the terrace that ran the length of the living room continued along the south wall of the bedroom.

Hearing Price approach, she jumped from the bed and went to stand by the French doors, her back to the room. She stood waiting for him to say something, but he didn't speak. He merely set their bags down and left. Amanda sighed, not knowing what to do next. How could she stay in this perfect lovers' hideaway for a week?

A few minutes later, he came back. This time, he leaned against the doorway, his tall frame filling the space. He had removed his jacket. His shirt was open at the collar and his sleeves were folded back to reveal his powerful forearms.

He could sense her turmoil. How could he not, when she had made her feelings about this marriage so clear? He had never doubted that she was in love with him, but he had decided long ago that that kind of love was something he no longer needed or wanted. So the first time they had made love, when he had discovered that she was a virgin, he had deliberately said things to hurt her. By using all the words he knew could wound her, he was sure he would eliminate any notions of a commitment or relationship she might have. Her innocence reminded him too much of a time when he had wanted all those same things. Only then, it was with Shelley that he had promised to share his life. Price winced at the memory, surprised he could still remember the pain.

Amanda continued to look through the glass panes to the darkness beyond, but what she saw was a reflection of the room behind her. 'I wish you hadn't brought me here,' she said softly. 'I don't think I can cope with all this.'

'This or me?' Price asked, his voice low and unhurried.

'It's all the same thing,' Amanda answered. Slowly, he crossed the room to stand behind her, so close that Amanda could feel the heat radiating from his body. Quickly she turned. 'Price,' she said feeling breathless, 'you know how I feel about this, us. Please don't...'

'I won't force you to do anything you don't want to do, Amanda, but I'll be damned if I'll spend my wedding night all alone,' he said tersely. 'Change your clothes while I build a fire.'

Amanda opened her suitcase and lifted out a silk nightgown and matching robe of palest pink. She had bought this for her wedding night, the only wedding night she would ever have, the only wedding night she had ever dreamed about having – with Price McCord.

Her heart raced as she changed, wishing that things were different, wishing she could forget all the things they had said to each other. She studied herself in the mirror, then spun around at the sound of his voice behind her.

'I've got a fire going and a bottle of champagne on ice,'

he said from the doorway as his eyes slowly travelled the length of her.

'Thank you,' she said in a small voice, fully aware of the way he was looking at her, 'but I think I'll stay here.'

'The living room or the bedroom, honey, it makes no difference to me, but we *are* going to spend the evening together.'

Swallowing with difficulty as she eyed the beautiful, inviting bed in the middle of the room, Amanda said, 'I'll be right out.'

'I thought you would,' Price said dryly.

Gathering her courage, Amanda retied the sash of her silk robe and, glancing once more at her image in the mirror, she decided that she looked...she didn't know how she looked! She thought her robe and gown were modest, or were they? Maybe it was the sensuous feel of silk against her bare skin that made her feel provocative.

The fire cast a seductive glow throughout the living room as it sent flickers of light and shadow in every direction. At the sound of rustling silk, Price turned from his place at the hearth, his breath catching sharply at the sight of her. With each step she took, he could feel his body change and respond to the breathtaking vision before him. Cast half in light and half in shadow, Price wondered if he would ever be able to control his desire for the woman before him. With supreme effort, he casually indicated the bottle of champagne and the two glasses he had set out on the low table in front of the sofa.

He poured the champagne, handed Amanda hers, then picked up his glass. Solemnly, he surveyed his beautiful bride over the rim. His eyes turned a dark turbulent blue, his expression serious. Amanda raised her eyes to meet his. With a nod he raised his glass in a silent toast to her.

In that instant, Amanda knew a desperate yearning for the man standing silent and inscrutable before her. She tried to find something to say to break the silence and diminish the desire that lay between them, but the words stuck in her throat. She felt hypnotised by his unwavering gaze and warmed by the heat radiating from the fireplace. The champagne relaxed her, and she wished that she didn't feel quite so mellow. Suddenly her knees felt as though they could no longer support her, and she sank on to the sofa behind her.

Price left his place and walked around behind her. With one hip resting on the back of the sofa, he lazily reached out and touched her hair, gently moving it aside. With the backs of his knuckles he lightly stroked her neck, just behind her ear. So soft.

Surely, I should have at least this. Forgetting entirely that the tension building between them could flare at any time, she allowed herself to luxuriate in the bliss of the moment, wanting to forget how dangerous and seductive he could be. What she didn't know was that she was as equally dangerous and seductive to him!

Sensing her reluctance to stop him, Price deftly began to massage the hollows where her shoulders met her neck. Then he leaned down and placed a soft kiss where only seconds ago his hands had been. It was so light that, for a moment, Amanda thought she might have imagined it. Until he kissed her again.

He felt her tense. When he leaned forward he saw the uncertainty on her face.

'Price...' she began.

His voice was lazy and sounded strangely detached. 'I told you earlier tonight that I wouldn't force you to do anything you didn't want to, Amanda. Your decision is obvious.' Then he let his hands fall away, straightened, then stood, abandoning her and his place on the back of the sofa.

'Price,' she cried softly, wanting to explain how she felt, but he turned away from her and went to the front door.

Amanda stood and watched him leave the house. At that moment, she felt uncertain and hurt. She wanted him as much as he wanted her, but there was too much that needed to be resolved between them. Why couldn't he understand that? She sighed and turned slowly toward the bedroom, taking her glass of champagne with her. She had only gone halfway when she turned and went back to the coffee table where she picked up the bottle of champagne and clutched it to her breast. As she silently padded toward the empty bedroom, she wished things could have ended differently tonight. Then she wondered how many nights ahead would end just as this one had.

In the bedroom, Amanda set her glass and the champagne on the table next to the bed. Then she took off her robe, pulled back the fluffy, snow-white duvet that covered the bed, and slid between the cool sheets. Then she reached for the champagne and refilled her glass. Of course, she knew she shouldn't be drinking anything at all. But this was her wedding night and it looked as though she was going to be spending it alone. *And that was exactly how she had intended it to be, wasn't it?*

She was already in bed when Price returned, so he put another log on the fire and poured himself a scotch and water. Stretching out on the sofa, he silently toasted himself for a botched wedding night. All he had had to do was tell her that he loved her, but he couldn't even do that. He downed his drink and reached for the nearby bottle. He poured another, this time not bothering with the water. Tugging at his shirt, he pulled it out of his trousers and began to undo the buttons. This was going to be a long night.

Price woke suddenly and for a moment he couldn't remember where he was. He looked at his watch, unable to make sense of the tiny reflective numbers there. The only light in the room was from the smouldering embers in the fireplace. He stretched his arms and his legs, feeling stiff and sore from lying on the sofa. Sitting up, he ran his hands over his face and tried once more to see the time. Then he remembered where he was and why. Mumbling to himself, he stood unsteadily.

'There's no reason for me to be uncomfortable when I have a perfectly good bed waiting for me,' he grumbled as he walked down the hallway to the bedroom. Then he remembered his beautiful-but-unwilling bride was also in the same bed. He thought about waking her, then decided against it. Plenty of time tomorrow, he thought. This situation could not go on forever – it couldn't even go on for one more night. He wouldn't be able to stand another night like tonight. There wasn't enough scotch in the world!

Amanda opened her eyes, winced, then closed them again. It was bright in the room, so bright she was unable to focus. Vaguely she wondered where she was and what time it was. Slowly she turned her head, and was assaulted by a sharp, stabbing pain behind her eyes. After a minute, she slowly opened her eyes again, then rubbed the back of her hand over her eyes in an effort to throw off the last traces of sleep, but her brain remained fuzzy. She shifted, then blinked rapidly. Her heart started to pound so hard she could feel it as she struggled to her elbows. Her stomach did a somersault, leaving her queasy.

What have I done? She moaned, not realising she had made a sound and tried once again to sit up. But before she could move any further, Price threw his leg across both of hers and at the same time grabbed both of her wrists, pinning them against the bed. His body covered most of hers and as she tried to squirm out from underneath him, she realised that her nightgown had ridden up around her hips.

'Oh, my God,' she moaned. His naked flesh was pressed against hers.

'Good morning, sweet girl,' he said softly, his face only a few inches from hers. Price knew he clearly had her at a disadvantage. Her face was slightly swollen with sleep and her lips were full and pink. He lowered his head and kissed her lightly. She was so beautiful with her dark shiny hair in disarray across the pillow.

'What are you doing?' she said slowly, her voice a little huskier than normal. 'Where are we?'

'We are exactly where we belong,' he smiled, kissing her once more. 'In bed – together.'

'At the beach,' she said, remembering.

'On our honeymoon,' he added, kissing her again, only longer this time.

'I want you to move,' Amanda hissed with as much effort as she could muster.

'Not a chance,' he answered.

Amanda tried to recall anything that might have happened after she had gone to bed last night, but all she remembered was how awful she felt, and how the champagne made her feel, if not less lonely, at least a little more righteous for spurning her husband's advances on their wedding night.

So why, then, was Price in bed with her? And why was he acting as though they had been intimate and he obviously was ready for more? They hadn't been, had they? Amanda begged her fuzzy brain to work. No, she would have remembered, even with the champagne she drank, she would never forget if they had...no, she could never forget something like that, could she? Just then, Price ran his other hand up her thigh. He was making her extremely nervous.

'I want to get up,' she said irritably, suddenly afraid she was going to be sick. 'I have to get up right now.'

'Uh, huh,' he said as he nuzzled her neck.

'Please, Price, I have to get to the bathroom.'

'Then you have to promise me you'll come back to bed,' he said as he rolled off her and watched as she quickly sat up, then grabbed her head with one hand and her stomach with the other, then raced to the bathroom.

Sitting up, Price propped his hands behind his head and waited. He knew Amanda wouldn't willingly return to bed. When she came out of the bathroom, he noticed how pale she looked.

With her eyes downcast, she reached for her robe then gingerly skirted the bed. Looking toward the scene beyond the French doors, she opened them wide, letting the cold morning air into the room and stepped outside.

Price wondered if she had had a bout of morning sickness. 'Are you OK?' he asked.

She nodded. She still couldn't remember anything that might have happened between them last night.

'Don't you want to spend the morning in bed with me?'

'No,' she answered primly. 'I'd like to go for a walk on the beach.'

'Aren't you going to ask me?' he said, sitting up straighter against the pillows.

She turned back toward him and she couldn't help but notice that the sheet was riding low on his hips. His body was big and hard and lean, and her temperature was rising just watching him. Unconsciously she reached to tuck her hair behind her ears while she chewed on her lower lip. 'Ask you what?'

'About last night.'

'Nothing happened last night,' she declared.

Price chuckled at her discomfort, his eyes never leaving hers. 'If nothing happened, then why do you suppose we slept in the same bed together?'

'I don't want to talk about it,' she answered as she headed for the bathroom once more, stopping only long enough to grab some clothes from her suitcase.

Minutes later, as she stood under the full force of the shower spray, Amanda was still puzzled. Surely if they had made love during the night she would have remembered. No, she decided, nothing happened. Nothing at all.

Price was still laughing at Amanda as he pulled on a pair of worn jeans and padded down the hall, first stopping in the bathroom then continuing on toward the kitchen.

Dressed except for her shoes, Amanda followed the smell of freshly brewed coffee. At the door to the kitchen, she stopped. Price was standing in front of the open fridge with one arm propped against the freezer and the other resting on the open door. Silently she feasted on the sight before her. The muscles in his back were contoured and smooth, his jeans rode low on his hips and delineated the shape of his buttocks and thighs. It was an altogether pleasing sight and unexpected flutters of excitement rippled through her. She felt wicked. She couldn't ever remember looking a man over that carefully and liking what she saw as much as she did now.

He was searching for something to fix for breakfast. Deciding that the fridge contained nothing worthwhile, he straightened and turned, surprised to find Amanda leaning against the framework of the door. Her hands were tucked in the front pockets of her jeans, her eyes intently assessing his anatomy.

Embarrassed at being caught staring at him, she guiltily lowered her eyes. He crossed the small kitchen unhurriedly and stood before her. She pulled her hands out of her pockets and was now nervously smoothing the still damp tendrils of hair away from her face. Without moving any closer, Price dipped both his hands inside the waistband of her jeans and pulled her close so that her breasts and pelvis pressed against him. Then he leaned over to reach her upturned face and kissed her.

Raising his head, he continued to study her. 'I hope

you're not hungry,' he said. 'There's nothing in the house for breakfast.'

Amanda shook her head, hardly able to concentrate on anything except the feel of his body against hers and the heat of his hands inside her jeans.

'We can go into town later to have lunch and pick up some groceries for tonight. I thought we could have dinner here unless you'd rather go out.'

Again Amanda shook her head. A rise in body temperature was causing her to feel a lassitude she couldn't shake off. All she wanted to do was to continue to experience the warm, hypnotic sensation that was spreading from her body to her brain.

Pulling his hands from the waistband of her jeans, he gave her a playful nudge. 'Here's your coffee. When you finish getting ready, we'll go for that walk.'

If he had thrown cold water on her, Amanda couldn't have been more startled. Automatically she reached for the cup he held out to her.

When she had finished the coffee, she said, 'I need to get my shoes and a sweater.'

'Grab one for me out of my bag,' Price said as she headed toward the bedroom.

In the bedroom, she looked suspiciously at the rumpled bed. *Had they...?* No, she thought, reinforcing her earlier decision. Definitely not. He was just playing games with her. She stooped to unzip Price's bag and then reached in to find his sweater, but her hand stilled as it came in contact with his clothes. She had never handled a man's clothes before. It seemed so personal. Picking up his sweater, she pressed it against her face, inhaling the scent, then clutched it against her.

'Did you find it?' asked Price from behind her.

'I, uh, didn't know if this was the one you wanted,' she answered without turning to look at him. 'I didn't want to mess your things up.'

'So I noticed,' Price said as he crossed the room and stooped down beside her. 'The one you have in your hands is fine.' He watched her pull a sweater from her bag. Then she stood and slipped it over her head. 'I've never seen you in a pair of jeans before.'

'You've never seen me in a lot of things,' she quipped.

'I'm not interested in seeing you in a lot of things. I prefer you without anything on.'

Amanda pushed past him and headed for the front door. She didn't know if she was blushing because of his remark, or if it was because he had caught her with his sweater pressed against her face.

Under a sunny but cold sky, the waves washed in hurriedly then slowly seeped away. The beach was deserted. It was too far into the winter for tourists and the only people in the area were those who lived there all year long. Only their voices broke the solitary, repetitive sound of water rushing toward the beach. They had walked for about a mile when Price stopped and caught Amanda's hand to keep her from going further.

'Let's turn back.'

She nodded in agreement, her hand remaining in his.

As they neared the house, Price turned to her. 'I'll race you to the house,' he said, suddenly feeling younger than he had in years.

'You're on,' she said, her eyes sparkling and her cheeks flushed from the cold air.

He beat her easily and as she ran toward him, he reached out catching her and swinging her around. 'Are you OK?'

'I'm fine,' she answered breathlessly.

'Are you sure?

'Yeah, why?'

'I forgot about the baby. You shouldn't be running like that.' Price's eyes were serious as he looked down at her.

She pushed against his chest to distance herself from

him. 'I'm fine,' she repeated, the sparkle no longer in her eyes. 'I can continue to do anything I feel like doing. Anything I would normally do.'

Realising that his concern had broken their light-hearted mood, Price let Amanda go and suggested they go on into town. During the short drive, both of them realised that they had problems to resolve before they could even hope to make this marriage work.

The mention of the baby had been sobering to both of them.

chapter fourteen

The town of Willow Beach, with a winter population of 1,745, was an unexpected treat for Amanda. Once a popular resort in the early 1900s, it had retained many of its original buildings and all of its charm. Progress had left it untouched when other resorts further down the coast had become fashionable.

Price and Amanda enjoyed a leisurely lunch at a small café, followed by a walk through the shops that made up Willow Beach's downtown. After a stop at the grocery store, where they debated the merits of one menu over another, they headed back to the house.

When they had finished putting the groceries away, Price insisted that Amanda rest for a while. She protested at first, then gave in. It felt so good to have someone show concern for her. As a compromise, she lay down on the sofa rather than going to the bedroom. She slept until she heard Price in the kitchen.

'I tried to be quiet,' he said, 'but kitchen things are so noisy.'

'I don't even remember falling asleep,' she said as she stretched, feeling refreshed. 'Isn't that strange?'

'From what I've read,' he said as he continued to rummage through the cabinets, 'the need for sleep is normal during the early stages of pregnancy.' He looked up just in time to see a look of dismay cross Amanda's face and wished he could have taken his words back. They had only served to remind her of the reason for their hasty marriage.

Seeking an excuse to gather her composure, Amanda went to freshen up. In the bathroom she splashed cold water on her face. As she dried off with a towel, she studied her reflection in the mirror. Twice today Price had reminded her about her condition and the real reason for their marriage. Was she being overly sensitive, becoming offended at what was nothing more than the reality of their situation? Was he genuinely concerned for her?

When she returned to the kitchen, she saw that Price had already started to make dinner. 'I'll make the salad,' she said and headed for the fridge.

Just as she stepped past him, he leaned down to check the oven, brushing against her. The small kitchen suddenly became even more crowded with the tension that flared between them. Amanda gathered what she needed from the fridge and moved past Price again, this time making sure not to touch him.

'This kitchen is too small for two people,' she muttered as she began to wash the lettuce.

He stepped past her to reach an overhead cabinet, touching her again. 'This kitchen is just right for two people. See?' he said as once more he scooted by, this time rubbing playfully against her. The air almost crackled.

Amanda knew he was deliberately teasing her and she was unsuccessfully trying to ignore him. Somehow they managed to cook dinner while she scrupulously tried to avoid contact with him, and he deliberately touched her as much as possible, everywhere. Each time there was contact on his part or evasion on hers, they laughed, making a silly game of it. It should have lessened the tension between them, and it did – but it also raised the stakes. Sooner or later, the chase would begin in earnest.

When dinner was ready, Amanda carried silverware, napkins and glasses to the coffee table since they had decided to eat in front of the fireplace. During dinner, they talked about what they had seen earlier in town, and about Price's surprising culinary talents.

'I didn't know you could cook,' Amanda said.

'I didn't either, until I was in high school and my mother decided that she was tired of being a stay-at-home mum. She became a travel agent and turned all her and Dad's friends into clients. I used to come home after school starving. It didn't take me long to figure out that there wasn't anyone there to fix me something to eat. No just-baked brownies or freshly iced cakes. So I had to fend for myself. After a while, I decided I liked to cook and, occasionally, I would have dinner ready by the time my parents got home from work.

'How about you?' he asked with a grin. 'Will cooking be a passion we can share?'

'Me? Cook? Not unless I absolutely have to. When my grandmother was sick, I cooked all the time – things I knew she would like. But it has always been a chore for me. So, no, we will not be sharing that kind of passion.'

'That's OK. There's always the other kind,' he said.

Amanda blushed. She should have detoured right around that one instead of plunging straight ahead. But it had been that kind of evening – teasing and playful. 'But it is nice to know I won't have to worry about it anymore.'

'The passion or the cooking?' His eyes sparked.

'Both,' she said.

When they had finished Amanda said, 'I'll clear the dishes away. It's the least I can do after that wonderful dinner.' She got to her feet and began picking up their plates off the coffee table.

'I'll help,' he said as he followed with the rest and began to load the dishwasher.

'I'm surprised someone hasn't tried to marry you before,' teased Amanda, her mood relaxed. 'Not only are you a good cook but you're willing to help clean up.'

Price turned just as Amanda tried to scoot around him. They collided. Price reached out and took hold of her arms to steady her. 'Someone did once,' he said. Then he pulled her toward him and wrapped his arms around her, knowing that he should tell her about Shelley. *Now.* Instead, he held her close and kissed her temple.

Without warning, the image of the woman at the wedding flashed across Amanda's mind. She wanted to question him, but she was caught up in the intense pleasure of being held by him. Instead, she wrapped her arms around him. In that moment, she knew without a doubt that this was where she wanted to be.

'Let's finish our wine,' he said as he guided her out of the kitchen, his arm around her shoulders while her head rested against his chest. He let her go only long enough to push the coffee table out of the way and pull some pillows from the sofa to the floor. Settling himself, he reached again for Amanda.

In silence, they sipped their wine. Sighing, Amanda snuggled closer. She stirred when she felt him bury his face in her hair, then she pulled away from him only long enough to search his face. What she saw there was a depth of longing so intense it was almost shocking. It was enough. She had lost her battle with Price and she knew it.

Effortlessly, he lifted her across his lap as her arms wrapped around his neck and her parted lips found his. She shifted in an effort to mould her body more closely to his, and as she moved she felt him growing hard against her. She moved against him again, this time slowly and deliberately.

'If you do that once more, this night could be the biggest disappointment of both our lives,' growled Price. Without warning he rolled her to the floor, his length following her, pinning her so that she was incapable of any significant movement beneath him.

Amanda giggled. 'It was such a fleeting moment of power.'

Her next sentence was forgotten as his lips travelled to the hollow at the base of her throat, and his hands deftly slipped the buttons of her blouse from their anchors. His lips followed the path blazed by his hands and with every inch of skin that he exposed, Amanda lost the rest of whatever reservations remained. Capturing her breast with his mouth, his tongue teased her nipple. In return, she reached for the part of him that had become insistent and throbbing.

The lovers' ritual that had begun with slow and sensual rhythms soon erupted into a raging fire fuelled by their passion. The intense desire to touch and taste the heat of bare flesh supplied the driving need to strip the few pieces of clothing that remained. Their pace was frantic now, the intensity of desire surpassing all else. Price fought for some measure of control as Amanda offered her waiting body to him, but he found none as she met each thrust with a passion and need that matched his own. With each motion, she felt a pressure within building higher and higher. No longer able to hold back, they sought release, exploding into waves of pleasure so intense as to be almost unbearable.

For long heart-stopping moments neither of them spoke, but roused only to touch, to reassure and to confirm that what they had shared was real.

Much later, when he carried her down the hallway to their room, Price knew that the time had come for him to be completely honest with her. Carefully, he laid her down on the bed, his eyes never leaving hers.

'You are everything I've ever wanted,' he whispered as he stretched out beside her, 'but there are some things you don't know about me.' He lay propped up on his elbow, the fingers of his left hand tracing lazy patterns across her breast and down her arm.

She reached out, her fingertips brushing against his face. 'You don't have to...' she began.

Quickly he covered her lips with his fingertips. 'I know,' he said softly, 'but there is something you need to hear first. This is difficult for me, Amanda. I've said and done some cruel things to you, things I regret. I suppose I was fighting what I felt for you. There are some things in my past that have caused me not to trust any woman. The kind of relationships I've had didn't require any trust. They were only a series of sexual encounters with no promises made and none expected. Caring for someone was not something I wanted any part of. Then you came along and I found myself thinking about things I hadn't thought about in years.' He turned his head away, his jaw tightened. 'I didn't like it at all. I was angry at you and at myself. I never wanted to be seriously involved with anyone again. There was someone a few years ago. It...' Price swallowed as if it hurt to talk. 'It didn't work out.'

Amanda reached up and smoothed his dark, rumpled hair.

He caught her hand with his and brought it to his lips.

'You don't have to tell me about it,' she whispered. 'We've got the rest of our lives to share our secrets. I don't want anything to interfere with what we have tonight. The past can wait for another time.'

He turned toward her. 'I love you,' he said, his voice husky. 'I've loved you for such a long time, but this is something you need to know. Something I should have told you before we were married.'

Before he could say more, Amanda reached out again to him. This time, she cradled his face between her hands and touched his lips with hers. 'Later,' she whispered, reluctant to let anything break this magical intimacy.

And so for the second time in only a few minutes, Amanda forestalled Price's efforts to tell her about his past – about Shelley. He was at once relieved, and as she began to do more than just kiss him, distracted. On some distant level, he resolved to set things straight between them before the week was out, before the honeymoon was over.

Now it was more important than ever that there be no secrets between them.

But the week passed too quickly in the lovely haze that only occurs during a romantic interlude when everything appears soft and unfocused and perfect. Later, Amanda would say that Price should have told her the truth in the very beginning, and Price would say that he had tried more than once.

For now, it was put aside and forgotten.

At Price's insistence, he and Amanda moved into his apartment. Soon he was going to begin renovations on the Hamilton-Sperry house. Once the work was finished, he and Amanda would move back there. Remembering Amanda's scathing comments about the decor of his apartment, Price suggested that she make whatever changes she wanted. Within a few weeks, the transformation was complete and Price was pleasantly surprised. With the addition of a few pieces of her antique furniture and, along with some colour, it took on a look that was warm, comfortable and inviting.

Pleased with the apartment's new look, Amanda invited Joan over for dinner. Price was out of town and wouldn't be back until the following day. Not only did she want to see Joan, she wanted to tell her about the baby. They were seated at the dining room table when Amanda made her announcement.

'You're pregnant? Already?' said Joan.

'More than already,' Amanda said, her face turning red. Tonight she was wearing jeans and an oversized sweatshirt, so her figure didn't give her away. 'The baby is due in May.'

'In May?' Joan repeated. 'But that's…'

Seeing the surprise on Joan's face, Amanda said, 'Don't bother counting backwards. I was two-and-a-half months pregnant when we got married.'

'You didn't tell me!'

'I didn't tell anyone, Joan. Not even Price. He found out by accident.'

Joan grinned. 'This may sound silly, but I used to worry about you. You were so uptight, so perfect. Now, finally, you did something really stupid – and absolutely wonderful!'

'Looking back, it was pretty stupid. But it's worked out OK.'

'You're married to a great guy like Price and it's just OK?'

Amanda grinned. 'Better than OK.'

'A lot better?' asked Joan teasingly.

'So good I can't believe it. Everyday I wake up and wonder what's going to happen today? What's out there that I don't know about that is going to come crashing down around my head and spoil all this incredible happiness? And you know what? Nothing happens! Each new day is better than the one before.'

So far Price had managed to side-step a number of social invitations, preferring instead to spend his evenings at home. He knew it was inevitable that they would soon have to accept some invitations, but he wanted to put it off as long as possible. For one thing, he wanted to give Amanda as much time as he could to feel secure in her new role as his wife. For another, he wanted to protect her from the gossip that would surely surface concerning the reason for their hasty marriage.

Already, he could detect the rounding of her hips and thickening of her waist. It was subtle, but it was there. Once her pregnancy began to show the reason for their hurried nuptials would be obvious to everyone. There would be speculation and undoubtedly some snide remarks. Price didn't care, and he knew that absolutely no one would make reference to this fact in his presence. But

Amanda was a newcomer, not one of them. And it was she who would be the most vulnerable. She was precious to him, and he wanted to do everything he could to protect her.

As the weeks passed he became, if it was possible, even happier. And the one thing that troubled him in the beginning – his failure to tell Amanda about Shelley – diminished in urgency with each passing day. Still, he knew that he would have to confide in her. When the time was right. When it would not upset the harmony they had so recently achieved. After all, it wasn't like he hadn't tried!

Tonight, Amanda was very much on his mind as he drove slowly through the early evening downpour. The skies were dark and cold and the rain battered the windshield in blinding sheets, rendering the wipers ineffective. Everywhere the streets were flooded. The rushing water from the sudden storm had caused many cars to stall.

As he parked the car and pulled the keys from the ignition, Price looked for Amanda's car, but it wasn't parked in its usual spot. In one calculated movement, he opened the car door and sprinted to their apartment. He was drenched from head to foot and cold, his clothes plastered to him. He unlocked the door, but there were no welcoming lights and no appetising smells coming from the kitchen. Instead, the apartment was dark and empty. Price walked quickly from room to room, turning on lights as he went.

First he worried that something had happened to her, then he was upset because she hadn't left him a note. In the kitchen, he reached for a towel and began to dry his face and his hair while he dialled Joan's number. Ten minutes later, he slammed the phone in its cradle. 'Damn!' he shouted in frustration. He had called everyone he could think of and no one had seen Amanda.

He stalked off to the shower and quickly peeled off his cold, clammy clothes. Then he turned on the hot water and stepped inside. He wasn't angry because she wasn't home; he was frantic because she was out driving in this weather.

He was in the kitchen pouring a drink when he heard the key turn in the lock. He charged into the hallway then stopped abruptly. Amanda had her back to him as she propped her dripping umbrella against the wall then reached for a hanger from the cupboard.

'Where the hell have you been.' It was a statement, not a question. Price's voice was low and cold, his fury barely controlled.

Amanda froze in mid-motion, the hanger in her right hand, her coat in the other. Rivulets of water ran down the fabric of her raincoat onto the tile floor. After a suspended moment, she began to move almost in slow motion. When she finished hanging her coat she turned, 'Hello, Price,' she said as she began walking toward the bedroom.

'Answer me.'

Amanda turned to face him. 'I had an appointment this afternoon.'

'With the doctor?' he asked.

'No, with an editor who happened to be in town. I'm going to do the illustrations for a new book.' Amanda waited for his reaction. She was furious but she refused to let him see how agitated she was.

He had not moved since he had first confronted her. 'There's no need for that. You're my wife now. You don't have to work.'

She couldn't believe what she was hearing. 'This has nothing to do with being your wife, Price. This has to do with being me.'

'It has everything to do with being my wife. Do you have any idea what our financial situation is? No, I guess you don't since we've never discussed this. Money is not a problem. I'll give you whatever you want.'

Amanda's temper flared. First, Price had forced her to marry him and now he wanted to control her every move.

'What I want, Price, is for you to let me be who I am. Besides, this is not some little job I do because I need something to occupy my time. This is who and what I am. I'm an artist, an illustrator, and I don't need your permission to continue my business. I've worked hard to build up my business and I'm not about to give that up.'

Amanda turned and walked toward the bedroom and as she reached the doorway she turned once more. 'And I don't give a damn if you or your snooty friends approve.'

Price downed the drink he had left on the kitchen counter, grabbed his jacket from the wardrobe and left, slamming the front door behind him.

Amanda lay on the bed and let her tears flow unchecked. They had been married less than a month. She should have known it would only be a matter of time before things came down to this. Mentally, she ran through every awful thing Price had done or said since she had met him, and she was gratified to know the list was long.

It was almost midnight and he still wasn't home. Reluctantly, Amanda got up from the bed and changed from her clothes into her nightgown, then crawled beneath the covers. She tried to stay awake so that she could listen for him when he came home, but within minutes she was sound asleep.

The room was bright when she awoke. She sat up, disoriented. It was ten in the morning. How could she have slept so late? It was obvious as she walked through the apartment that Price had come home sometime during the night. She looked to see if he had left a note, but he hadn't.

As the day progressed, she found it difficult to concentrate on her work. Finally, she put her pencils and pens away and went for a long walk. This was their first argument since the honeymoon. Right now, she didn't quite know what she would say to Price when he came home.

At six that evening, Price let himself in and closed the door behind him. In the kitchen, Amanda was cooking dinner. Even though she had her back toward him, she heard him approach and her heart beat a little faster.

'Something looks good,' he said casually.

'You mean smells good,' she replied without turning.

'No,' he said as he crossed the kitchen to pull her back against him and wrap his arms around her. 'I meant what I said.'

She turned in his arms and put her arms around his waist.

He leaned down to kiss her then pulled back to look at her. 'I was worried about you last night because you weren't home and the roads were so bad.' His eyes were a dark, troubled blue.

'I know,' Amanda answered as she nibbled at the side of his neck.

'If you want to keep working, it's OK with me,' Price said as he buried his face in her hair.

'I know,' Amanda said again. 'Isn't it nice that your plans coincide with mine?'

'I thought you didn't like to cook,' he said looking over her shoulder toward the stove.

'I don't,' she replied.

'Can dinner be put on hold for a while?'

Amanda looked back at the stove. 'Not unless there's a good reason.'

His laugh was muffled as he lowered his head and whispered in her ear, and Amanda knew it would be much later than usual when they finally got around to dinner.

chapter fifteen

The Christmas holidays arrived and departed much too quickly, but they were some of the happiest Amanda could remember. She and Price spent Christmas Eve at home alone. After dinner, they exchanged their gifts in front of the tree.

Price's gift to Amanda was a set of blueprints for an addition to the house. She was surprised and touched. She knew all about the work on the house that was in process, but there had never been any mention of an addition. The plans showed the removal of the existing kitchen wall and the addition of a family room and separate studio for Amanda, complete with its own cosy corner fireplace, bookshelves, and a wall of French doors that would lead to a brick patio. It was exactly what she had visualised.

'Just think, the next Christmas we have together will be in our own home. I want to have a big family dinner there on Christmas Day,' she said.

'That's a lot of work for a woman who doesn't like to cook,' Price said.

'Oh, honey, I wasn't planning on cooking. That would be your job. You're the one with all the culinary talent. I'll just play the role of gracious hostess,' she said, still disbelieving the wonderful turn her life had taken. She was married to Price, the man she had dreamed of since she was fifteen. Soon they would have a baby and the three of them would live in the most wonderful house in the world.

'Next Christmas, we'll also be playing Santa and Mrs Claus,' Price said.

'Will you be happy?' she asked. The change in him had been so unexpected that she sometimes wondered if his enthusiasm for his impending fatherhood was real or an act he put on for her benefit.

'I will be happier than you can imagine.' He leaned over and pulled her close to him and rested his hand on her rounded tummy. 'I can't wait for our baby to be born.'

Amanda blinked rapidly to hide her sudden tears and smiled at him before planting a quick kiss on his cheek. 'Now I have to get your present,' she said, scooting toward the tree. She pulled out a large flat box and handed it to him shyly.

It was a large framed watercolour she had painted for him, a soft rendering of the boats docked at Willow Beach. 'Next to you, this is the best gift I've ever received,' he said. The watercolour reminded him of Amanda, delicate to the eye but far more resilient than one would expect.

Christmas Day was a joyful affair at Kate and Ed's, with Mike and Caroline, Louise, and a few friends. Just being surrounded by all these loving people made Amanda feel that she was truly part of this family. The warmth and the happiness of that day seemed to erase all the loneliness and sadness that had hovered over her for so long.

The weeks turned into months and Price and Amanda developed a pattern that suited them both. Price left for the office early every day and Amanda was always up to see him off. She resumed her freelance work and made it a point to schedule any appointments so she would be home about the same time as Price. On weekends, they would drive out to the house to check the progress the contractors were making.

Together they began to make plans around the birth of their baby. Since the three of them couldn't live comfortably in the apartment, they made plans to move into the old house as soon as possible. Price was pushing hard to get the inside work completed before the baby was born, but there was still so much that needed to be done. The timetable for completing the outside work would be dictated by how much it rained during the coming months.

Frequently, Amanda reflected on the changes in her life. She was incredibly happy. Kate and Ed treated her like another daughter. To Amanda, they were the parents she had lost. She knew she would always be able to count on them. Caroline and Mike had become her friends, and she often had trouble reconciling the Caroline she now knew with the same brassy woman who had once barged into her home demanding to use the phone. The two women talked a lot about Amanda's pregnancy, and Caroline confided that Mike wanted to start a family soon, but she wanted to wait a while.

Price was everything Amanda had dreamed of. The only disturbing thing in her life was how quickly she had lost her figure. She complained a lot about how fat she was getting. Unfortunately, all she could do about it was exercise and watch her diet. Since January, she hadn't been able to fit into her regular clothes. But instead of donning maternity clothes, she bought clothes in larger sizes and with elastic waists, and she secretly complimented herself on how clever she was.

Occasionally Price teased her, but he knew that the fact that she looked obviously pregnant so soon after their marriage disturbed her. But he didn't share any of her concern over her size. Not only was he delighted that he was, at last, going to be a father, the rest of the McCord family were equally excited at the thought of a baby in their midst.

It was only when they received an invitation to the Atlanta Charities Cotton Ball to be held in April that Price became apprehensive. Because several of the banks that financed his real estate developments were sponsors, it was imperative that he and Amanda attend. Yet the last thing he wanted to subject Amanda to was this kind of scrutiny. In his bachelor days, his name had found its way on to many guest lists. Now that he was no longer single, everyone would be curious to meet his new wife.

When Price asked Amanda if she wanted to attend, she replied unexpectedly that she thought it might be fun, but she didn't have anything to wear. Price was caught off-guard. He had expected her to protest because of her now very obvious condition. What Price didn't know was that at seven-and-a-half months into her pregnancy, Amanda had never in her life been happier or felt more loved and secure.

Caroline was delighted that Amanda had asked her to help shop for a dress for the occasion. It was understood that Amanda wanted to find a dress that was as flattering as possible. Late one afternoon, as they relaxed over coffee, Caroline and Amanda agreed on two things. The first was that they were both tired, having been to every store in town. The second was that they had found the perfect dress for Amanda to wear to this important event.

Three weeks later, on the day of the ball, Amanda decided that she would concentrate only on making herself look as pretty as a pregnant woman now in her eighth month could. Actually, she was not as big as she felt even though her due date was getting close. While some women do not take to pregnancy well, Amanda glowed. Her skin and hair had a glossy, healthy look and to Price she was even more beautiful than before.

Amanda had just finished her hair and make-up and was about to slip on her dress when Price, fresh from the shower, walked into the bedroom. A white towel, wrapped and anchored low and inviting on his hips, caused Amanda to look him over appreciatively.

Catching her eyes on him Price teased, 'Pregnant women aren't supposed to cast lecherous glances at partially-clothed men.'

'Oh? Are there any better kind of men to look at?' she asked innocently.

'Naked men,' he answered as he playfully whipped off the towel he was wearing. 'Now, if you would just come on over here we could get down to some serious business.'

'I'm afraid I'm going to have to postpone any business with you until after your child decides to put in an appearance, if he or she ever does. I'm beginning to think I'm going to have a baby elephant – and it's going to take two years.'

'I can't wait two years to make love to you again,' he said as he pulled Amanda close and put his arms around her.

'Me neither,' whispered Amanda. 'I love you too much.'

Price put his hands to her shoulders setting her back slightly, then turned her and smacked her playfully on the buttocks. 'Get away from me, you sinful woman,' he said in his best riverboat gambler imitation, 'and see to making yourself the most beautiful woman at the Cotton Ball.'

'Sir, you must mean the fattest woman at the ball,' replied Amanda in her overly exaggerated southern accent.

'No, I mean the most beautiful,' he said, his voice serious, all trace of teasing gone.

'Thank you,' she whispered as she turned and reached for her new dress before he could see the glitter of tears in her eyes.

Throughout their marriage, Price had done everything possible to let Amanda know how much he loved her and how desirable she was to him. Life with her had made him realise how much time he had wasted in shallow, meaningless liaisons. The only cloud over their otherwise sunny relationship was the guilt he sometimes felt for not having told Amanda the truth about Shelley.

Of course, he could always justify this because on their honeymoon she had stopped him from explaining everything to her, but he knew that even then he had waited too long. He should have told her everything before they got married. Now time was running out. He couldn't put it off much longer. He had to tell her. He was not going to let anything interfere with their happiness when the baby was born. Resolving to get it behind him, Price decided that he would take Amanda out for a late brunch the following morning. He would tell her then.

The glitter of the hotel ballroom was surpassed only by the glitter of those in attendance. It was Atlanta's biggest social event of the year and, as such, it attracted only the brightest stars of business, politics and entertainment. This was the setting for Amanda's belated introduction into Atlanta society.

Tonight she was outstanding in her elegant black dress with its pattern of bugle beads that covered the bodice and the sleeves. The simple lines of the black skirt that gathered below her breasts and fell in soft folds to the floor did not hide her stomach, but neither did they accentuate it.

Price was careful to stay with her throughout the evening. It was only when he was pulled away from their group by the president of one of the largest banks in the southeast that Amanda was left alone. Looking back over his shoulder as he walked away, Price was gratified to see that she was deep in conversation with several people.

Her confidence was growing and she was surprised to find she was actually enjoying herself. Price had been gone for about ten minutes when suddenly everyone around her stopped talking. Amanda, startled by the sudden silence, looked questioningly at the woman she had been talking with, then her eyes darted to those around her. All conversation had ceased. Words were frozen in mid-sentence.

Following the sudden shift of attention, Amanda looked over her shoulder, her gaze falling on the newcomer to the group. She recognised her immediately from her brief appearance their wedding reception. It was Shelley – the woman who had kissed Price so intimately.

It was impossible to say how long the silence lasted. Finally, it was broken by the blonde with the piercing green eyes when she stepped toward Amanda and said, 'We've never met. I'm Shelley Van Gordon, the ex-Mrs Price McCord.'

chapter sixteen

Amanda dimly remembered the sound of glass crashing at her feet and a kaleidoscope of lights all around her. She had no memory of the fall that followed.

Nor did she see the absolute look of satisfaction on Shelley Van Gordon's face upon seeing Price's stricken expression when he spun around to see his pregnant wife crumple to the floor.

Following that, for one split second, Price raised his head. The concern on his face had been replaced by a look of hatred – and it was aimed straight at Shelley.

Later, when she was being examined by a doctor in one of the hotel's rooms, Amanda thought whimsically that this had been as good a place as any to faint. There were always so many doctors at these functions that one could always be assured of prompt medical care. It was a lot better than sitting in a waiting room for hours. Then she remembered what had caused her to faint in the first place.

Was their marriage a sham? Based on lies? No, no, there had to be some logical explanation. But how could Price have kept something that important a secret? If he loved her, wouldn't he have told her the truth?

Amanda felt hurt and, worst of all, betrayed. Slowly, deliberately, she drew a protective shell around her and her baby, vowing she would never let Price McCord hurt her again.

It was only when her body convulsed and pain, more intense than anything she had ever before experienced, ripped through her that she forgot what had just taken place. The pain started in her lower back and radiated uncontrollably through her swollen abdomen. She cried out.

Price hovered nearby, frantic, helpless. Silently, he cursed himself for bringing Amanda here. He should have known that Shelley would be present and would use this opportunity to confront Amanda. But, right now, the most important thing was Amanda. If she or their baby was hurt, he would never forgive himself. Never.

The doctor motioned for Price to join him in the outer room. 'Your wife has gone into labour. You need to get her to the hospital right away. Call her doctor and have him meet us there. I'll follow you. She and the baby should be fine, but there's no need to take any chances.'

Price nodded, then reached for the phone. In all his life he had never felt so helpless – or so guilty.

Six-and-a-half hours later, Price McCord became a father. The tiny baby girl, Margaret Kathleen McCord weighed barely six pounds and was perfect in every way. The doctor reported that the mother was doing fine. Physically that was true, but the doctor had no way of knowing that Amanda's joy at giving birth to a beautiful, healthy baby was tempered by severe emotional complications.

The coffee in the plastic cup was cold and bitter. Price was tired. He ran his hand over his face and could feel the stubble of his beard grind coarsely against his palm. He had been so worried, even though the doctor kept reassuring him all during Amanda's labour that the baby was fine and the birth was progressing normally.

Then he smiled. Tonight he had become a father. He and Amanda had a baby girl, the most beautiful baby in the world. She had only been minutes old when he had held her in the delivery room. He thought his heart would burst with love.

But his joy at this miracle was overshadowed by his worry over Amanda. She had held his hand tightly and cried when the nurse placed the baby in her arms. But what would her reaction to him be now that she knew about Shelley? Oh God, what a mess he had made. He needed to explain things, to make Amanda understand why he hadn't told her the truth.

Price threw the coffee cup in the trash and walked down the hall past the nurses' station to his wife's room. The halls were quiet. Outside it was still dark, but soon the sun would rise, signalling the beginning of a new day, and he wondered what was in store for him and Amanda. The door to her room was partially open and as he pushed it open further, he halted at the sight before him. Amanda was propped up in bed with their baby cradled in her arms. The expression on her face was one of love and amazement and devotion. Darting out from beneath the pink blanket in her arms were tiny fists and feet that waved in the air.

Amanda looked up and her eyes met his. For a moment, the only movement in the room was that of the baby. Then Price walked over to the bed and sat on the edge. He looked at his wife, then down at his daughter. A perfect, tiny face stared seriously at him, her eyes the same dark blue as her father's, her hair just as dark as his.

'She's got a lot of hair for a newborn baby,' he said softly.

Amanda looked down at her infant daughter. 'She looks just like you.'

Price leaned toward Amanda as he rearranged the blanket around the baby, then ran his hand softly along Amanda's temple and down her cheek. 'Amanda, honey, I'm so sorry for not telling you. I'm sorry things happened the way they did tonight. I never meant to hurt you.'

Amanda shook her head slightly and looked away sadly. *Tonight.* It seemed like a hundred years ago. So much had happened in the hours since – the shocking discovery that her husband had been married before, followed by the premature birth of their baby.

Just then, tiny Meg McCord whimpered and Amanda unexpectedly held her out to her father.

He reached out to take the baby. His hands felt as though they were ten times their normal size. 'She is so beautiful,' he whispered as he pulled her towards him, cradling her against his chest.

Amanda saw the tenderness that radiated from his face as the baby wrapped her perfectly formed little hand around Price's index finger, and her heart ached for all of them. They had come so far together, only to be torn apart again.

As if he had read her thoughts, Price's expression turned sad. 'Honey, we have to talk about this, about what happened tonight. We can't let it come between us. We're a family now.'

Amanda's eyes glittered with tears. 'Not now, please. I...I need some time to think things over. I'm so tired.'

'I know,' he said and his heart ached as he kissed her gently. 'When you're feeling better, we can talk.' Nothing mattered now but Amanda and their baby. He would do anything to make things right between them.

The next morning, a giant teddy bear peeked around the door to Amanda's room. 'Is this where I can find the world's most beautiful baby?' the bear asked in a gruff voice.

'Of course,' answered Amanda.

Joan pushed the huge fluffy bear into the room and deposited it in a chair. She reached out to hug Amanda. Then, with both hands, she reached for the sleeping baby.

'Can I?' she asked in a whisper.

'Well, since you are her Aunt Joan you had better get used to holding her. I may want you to baby-sit.'

'Oh, Amanda, she's so little and so beautiful.'

'I think she looks like Price, don't you?' asked Amanda. A look of sadness crossed her face. It was ironic that at a time when she should have been happiest, she felt like her life was falling apart.

'Honestly, I can't tell who she looks like, except her hair is the colour of Price's,' Joan said as she looked down at the baby in her arms. 'Hey, sweet girl,' whispered Joan. 'When you come to stay with me, I'll give you all the cookies and ice cream you want. We won't tell your mummy, OK?'

After a few minutes, Joan said, 'I have some news of my own. I know you're going to find this hard to believe, but I'm getting married.'

'Married?' repeated Amanda. 'Oh, Joan, that's wonderful! When?'

Frantically, she tried to remember a name that Joan might have mentioned, but nothing came to mind. Then she realised that since her own marriage, she had been so preoccupied with Price and her own pregnancy that she hadn't kept in close touch with her friend.

'In December and, in case you're wondering,' Joan said dryly, 'it's Charlie. You met him the night we all went out for your birthday. Charlie with the glasses...'

'Charlie?' said Amanda. 'That Charlie? Your neighbour?'

Joan's face turned the same bright red as her hair. 'He's a lot different from the men I used to go out with, but he's wonderful and sweet and funny.'

'Oh, Joan, I'm so happy for you,' said Amanda as she held out her arms to hug her friend. For the next half-hour, Amanda listened to Joan's wedding plans, plans which included her as the matron of honour.

In the recesses of her mind, Amanda couldn't help but reflect on how suddenly her own happiness had disappeared. Here was her best friend, so happy about her coming marriage. It was only a few short months ago that Amanda had been just as happy. Even though the marriage had got off to a rocky start, it had recovered its footing and had definitely showed signs that it could endure for a lifetime. Until it had cracked and broken.

Less than twenty-four hours later, Amanda was busy packing the baby gifts she had received and was getting ready to leave the hospital. The time to face reality had arrived. She was so deep in thought that she didn't hear Price come into the room.

'Amanda?'

She paused, clutching the soft fabric of her baby's blanket in her hands. Then she raised it to her face, inhaling the sweet new smell. She turned.

'Ready to go home?' Price asked. His smile was tentative.

'Oh, Price.' She couldn't hide the sadness she felt.

His smile faded. 'Let's take our baby and go home, Amanda. We can talk there in private. We're a family – we love each other. We belong together. I know we can sort this out.'

Without moving, Amanda looked up into his eyes. Her voice was full of sadness when she said, 'I've thought about us, and I'm not going home with you. I want you to take me to your mother's. I'm going to stay there for the next few days until I'm able to take care of Meg and myself.'

Price was silent for a long moment. He felt like he had been kicked in the stomach. In spite of everything that had happened between them, he had never considered the possibility that Amanda and the baby wouldn't come home.

When he spoke, his voice was low and ragged. 'There's no need for that. Mum can come over to the apartment during the day to help with the baby.' He was bluffing and he knew it. He had gambled that he would be able to make things right with Amanda. Now he knew he had jeopardised the only thing in his life that really mattered.

He took a deep breath. 'Amanda, I should have told you about Shelley long ago,' he said, his voice deep and rough. 'I tried to tell you right after we were married.'

'How about before we were married?' she asked. 'Why didn't you tell me then? Do you have any idea what a shock it was to have an absolute stranger walk up to me and announce that she had once been married to my husband?' Amanda's eyes filled with tears. 'How could you do something like that to me? Didn't I deserve better than that from you? Why couldn't you have told me the truth?' This last was punctuated with sobs.

'It wasn't what you think, honey.'

'Were you married to her, Price?' she whispered.

'Yes.'

'When?'

'Four years ago.'

'I see,' she said, drawing a deep, shaky breath.

'No, you don't see. You're upset, and I understand that, but this is not the time to make any rash decisions,' said Price. 'I want you to know the whole story.'

'I'm afraid it's a little late for that. If you don't want to take the baby and me to your parents' house, I can take a taxi.'

'That won't be necessary,' Price said, his voice low.

Of all the things he had expected, this was not one of them. He had never for a moment believed that this was something that he and Amanda couldn't get through. All marriages had their problems, and the good ones lasted. When two people loved each other, they tried to work things out, didn't they? His throat ached with hurt and when he swallowed, it tasted strangely like bile.

When Amanda was settled with the baby in the guest room at his parent's house, Price went downstairs to the kitchen to fix himself a drink. It was only two in the afternoon.

'Don't you think it's a little early for that, Price?' asked his father.

Kate turned from the stove to face the two men.

'No, I don't,' Price answered tersely. 'But if it bothers you, I can go somewhere else to have it. I think I have a pretty good idea of how the both of you feel about me and this situation.'

Kate and Ed looked across the kitchen at each other. They knew about the incident at the Cotton Ball with Shelley.

From across the kitchen, Kate spoke. 'Honey, we're not taking sides. Whatever is wrong between you and Amanda is your business. Amanda asked us if she could stay here until she was able to take care of the baby. She has no place else to go, Price, and that's our grandchild.' Kate's voice quivered and her eyes filled with tears. Inside, her heart filled with pain for this grown son of hers. He had acted foolishly, but she knew he was hurting too.

'You did what you felt you had to,' Price said coldly.

Ed, who had been watching the interplay of words between mother and son, slammed his coffee cup down so hard that it set the saucer teetering back and forth on the table. 'I've just sat here and listened to the two of you waltz around the issue of why Amanda is here with us and not at home with you, Price, where she belongs. And I think it's time somebody faced some hard facts. Why the hell didn't you tell her you were married before? That's not the kind of secret you can keep from your wife. Didn't you realise that when Shelley showed up at your wedding she was hell-bent on causing trouble?'

'On second thoughts,' said Price, 'I believe I would enjoy that drink much more someplace else.'

'Oh, Price, no,' pleaded Kate as Price turned and walked out of the kitchen.

'Let him go, Katie,' said Ed. 'He's a damn fool.'

When Price had left the bedroom earlier, Amanda had looked down at the tiny bundle that lay beside her. She had thought that she would never again feel as great a sadness as she had when her grandmother died. Now she knew she was wrong. This was much, much worse – a degree of sadness so great as to cause excruciating pain deep in her heart. She doubted it would ever go away.

Price spent the rest of the afternoon and evening trying to drink himself into a stupor. It hurt too much to think, and yet no matter how much alcohol he consumed, he couldn't seem to dim the pain. He knew his own stupidity had caused him to lose the only woman he had ever loved, and the baby he so desperately wanted.

It was nearly a month later when Amanda moved out of the guest room and into a place of her own. She had wanted to move sooner, but Ed and Kate had insisted she stay. Finally, with Caroline and Mike's help, she was able to arrange to move back to her old apartment. It had been vacated a week earlier.

Ed had offered to get anything she wanted from the apartment she and Price had shared. But all Amanda wanted was her drawing board and art supplies, along with Meg's baby bed and chest. She bought a new sofa that folded out into a bed for herself, and a few pots and pans for the kitchen. She would add other things later when she felt better. Caroline phoned every day, and stopped by to see her and the baby every few days.

More than a month-and-a-half after their exchange in the kitchen, Ed and Price had still not spoken to each other. Price had continued to stop by his parents' house to see Meg, but only when he knew that his father would be away. During those times, Amanda remained out of sight. During his visits, Kate continued to urge her son to make things right with Amanda. Price would always remind his mother that Amanda had made her decision. He hadn't seen his wife since she had left the hospital. He had wanted to, desperately, but she had refused. So he waited, giving her the time she wanted, knowing he wouldn't be able to walk away from her again.

A week later, Ed was the first one to break the silence and set the gears in motion when he stormed into Price's office. It was late on Friday afternoon. 'I told your mother you were a damn fool,' Ed said without preamble as he slammed the door of Price's office behind him, 'but I never actually believed I was right.'

Price looked up from the stack of papers on his desk, startled by his father's abrupt entrance.

'Amanda's leaving town and she's taking the baby with her,' said Ed.

'What?' said Price rising. 'What are you talking about?'

'I'm talking about your wife – who has just announced that she has accepted a job offer in New York. And it's your baby, my only grandchild, that she is taking with her.'

Price was first speechless, then furious. 'How did you find out?' he asked his father as he turned and reached into the credenza behind his desk.

'She told your mother at lunch today, and your mother is at home crying her eyes out because she won't be able to see little Meg anymore. And I'm here to tell you,' continued Ed, 'that if Amanda and Meg mean anything to you at all, you'd better get off your ass and do something about it. Now!'

Price jumped from his chair, gave it a hard shove and headed for the door.

'None of this would have happened if you had been honest with Amanda in the first place,' Ed shouted to a now empty office.

A sentence ago, Price had left on the run, a large manila envelope in his hand.

chapter seventeen

Fifteen minutes later, Price slammed on the brakes in front of Amanda's apartment. It had been nearly two months since he had seen her. He had tried several times when she had been staying at his parents' house, but each time she had refused. So he would console himself by holding his baby daughter and telling her that sooner or later he would be able to patch things up with her mummy.

But, evidently, her mummy had other ideas.

His insistent banging on the door of Amanda's apartment was answered by a man dressed only in a pair of jeans and a T-shirt. His abundant light brown hair was rumpled like he had just got out of bed, and his feet were bare. He appeared to be in his late twenties.

'Yeah?'

Without answering, Price pushed past him into the apartment. 'Who are you?'

'John Brooks.'

'Where's Amanda? And what the hell is going on here?'

'That depends. What do you want with her?' John asked calmly. Just then a baby cried. He turned and went into the bedroom, then returned moments later with a small wiggling bundle in his arms.

'I'm Price McCord, Amanda's husband.'

The baby whimpered again.

'My, my,' said John in a soft voice to the baby he was holding. 'It appears your daddy has finally come for a visit.'

Amanda hurried up the stairs carrying a bag of groceries. She had been gone longer than she expected, and she hoped John had remembered to give Meg her bottle. John Brooks had been her neighbour when she had first moved to the apartment. Now that she was back, he had offered to watch the baby when Amanda needed to run errands. In return, Amanda had fixed dinner for him. They enjoyed each other's company but nothing more.

John was a writer and taught several classes at the community college. He was bright, articulate, and handsome. Had things been different, he might have asked her out, but he knew Amanda was still in love with her husband.

She called out to John, letting him know she was back. Then she looked up and stopped dead in her tracks. Price was seated on the sofa with Meg cradled in the crook of his left arm. In his right hand, he held a bottle.

'Hello, Amanda.'

She was speechless. Out of the thousands of times she had thought about where and when she would see him again, she had never ever conjured up a scene like the one before her.

Price ran his eyes over her, noting how thin she was.

'I can finish feeding her,' she said when she was able to speak. She hurried into the kitchen, deposited her groceries on the counter then returned.

'Where's John?' asked Amanda, noticing his absence for the first time.

'He left. He suddenly remembered something he needed to do. Get your things together, Amanda, and get anything Meg might need. As soon as she finishes her bottle, she's going to Grandma and Grandpa McCord's house to spend the night. You and I are going home by ourselves to try and work some things out.'

'But I...' Amanda's protest died on her lips. He was asking for a chance to explain, something she had stubbornly denied him since Meg's birth.

Ten minutes later, Price helped Amanda strap Meg

safely into her car seat. Several times, their hands touched and she felt the same tingle she had always felt whenever he was around. In the time they had been apart, she had missed him terribly. Many times since their separation she had wanted to call a halt to their estrangement, but her wilful pride had kept her from it. Now her heart was beating so hard against her chest that it actually hurt. Her hands were clammy.

Price started the car. As he pulled away from the curb he turned and looked at her. 'What's this I hear about you taking a job in New York?'

Amanda looked up, surprised.

'You can't take Meg. It would break my parents' hearts.'

'Would it break your heart too, Price?' she asked.

'You know damn well it would.'

'Then it's a good thing you came to see me. I would have never known that.'

'Cut it out, Amanda. I'm not the one who set up the barriers between us.'

With a nod she acknowledged his point, then she returned to the subject at hand. 'I don't know anything about a job in New York.'

'You don't?'

'No. Where did you hear that?'

'From Dad. He said you told Mum at lunch today.'

'I didn't have lunch with your mother today,' replied Amanda. 'Why would your dad say something like that?'

'I don't know,' answered Price. But of course he did.

'Wait here,' Price said when he pulled into the driveway of his parents' house. Quickly he gathered up the things Amanda had packed for Meg. Then he settled his daughter in the crook of his free arm and hit the doorbell with his elbow. Almost simultaneously, the porch lights flashed on and the front door opened.

'Hi, Mum,' he said while handing Meg over to her, then leaned down to plant kisses on his daughter's forehead and his mother's cheek.

'What a nice surprise, honey,' said Kate, 'but where did you get Meg?'

'Never mind,' he said. 'Meg wants to spend the night with her grandparents. Here's all her stuff. Where's Dad?'

'Right here,' answered Ed as he walked up behind Kate. When he saw Meg, he reached out to take her. 'How's my sweet little girl?' he asked in a soft voice that adults reserve for very small babies.

'Your little girl is fine,' answered Price.

Ed cleared his throat. 'Where's Amanda?'

'Out in the car. We're going home to talk about that job in New York – the one she knows absolutely nothing about,' said Price.

Ed looked down sheepishly. 'Now, Price, I only…'

'Cut it out, Dad.'

Ed looked up quickly.

Price grinned. 'There's evidently no end to what loving parents will do for their stubborn children. Thanks, Dad,' said Price, reaching out to grasp his father's shoulder.

'Anytime, son.'

Price jogged back to the car, anxious now to get to their apartment. He only hoped he could make things work. He had to make Amanda understand why he had never told her about his marriage to Shelley.

Darkness had fallen and the night seemed to weave a cocoon of intimacy around them. When they arrived at the apartment, Price opened the door then switched on the lamp in the living room. Amanda looked around curiously. She wasn't sure what she had expected. Nothing had changed, but it seemed as if she had been away a lifetime.

He headed for the kitchen. A few minutes later, he returned with a glass of wine in each hand. After handing one of the glasses to Amanda, he took the chair that faced her. He didn't trust himself to sit close to her, not until he got through this ordeal.

'Before I begin, there's something I want you to have. I was going to give this to you the day that you and Meg came home from the hospital,' said Price. He held out the large envelope he had taken from his office earlier in the afternoon.

Amanda looked up at him. His dark blue eyes held hers steadily until she reached across the space that separated them and took the envelope from his outstretched hand. With her head bent, she opened it and withdrew several sheets of paper. She began to read. After a few seconds, she realised the significance of what she held in her hands. It was a deed transferring the ownership of the Hamilton-Sperry house, along with the fifty acres that went with it, from Price McCord to Amanda Hamilton McCord.

'I...' Tears clouded her eyes. She took a deep breath and bit her lip. 'I don't know what to say.' She looked down at the papers in her hands once more. 'You don't have to do this, Price. I never expected...'

'I know that,' he said. It was one of the things he had found most endearing about her. She never expected him to give her things. But what she had expected from him — honesty and truthfulness — he had failed to give her. Now he had to mend this terrible break between them.

'No matter what the outcome of tonight, you and Meg will always have a home. I never really planned to live there alone, you know. Not even after I bought it. I would ride out there sometimes on the weekend and then I would realise that without you there, the house meant nothing.'

He got up from his chair, too restless to sit any longer. He walked to the window and stood with his back toward her. As difficult as it had been, he had just handed her something that would make it easier than ever for her to leave him. If she stayed with him now, he knew it would be because she wanted to. He had given her the freedom to choose, and that scared the hell out of him.

Amanda could tell how difficult this was for him, but she still hurt. It was that hurt that prevented her from going to him now and putting her arms around him. She had missed him terribly, but there were still secrets between them.

When he finally began to speak, Price's voice was low and sombre.

chapter eighteen

'I should have told you about Shelley a long time ago,' Price said. He paused, took a deep breath and went on. 'We were together for nearly two years. At first, we agreed that we didn't want anything more than just a good time, no commitments. Then, after the first year, she started pressuring me to get married. For me, it wasn't even an issue. I told her I wasn't ready to get married. She was disappointed, then after a while she seemed OK with it, although I knew it didn't make her happy. Another few months went by. She was busy with her career and I was just beginning to put the Cumberland River deal together.'

He stopped, then swallowed as if it still hurt to talk about it.

'She still talked about getting married, but by this time I was wondering if Shelley and I really belonged together. She wanted so much. Emotionally, she wanted my complete attention to every little bump and twist in her life. I was supposed to smooth things over for her. Professionally, she used every contact I had to further her career in real estate, and ruined some friendships along the way. I suppose she saw me as her entrée into Atlanta's high society, although I was only on the fringes. I was single, and an extra man is always in demand at social functions. That, and my grandmother had been a Davenport before she married. That was back before they lost all their money. But still, the name opened a lot of doors for me.

'Shelley wanted everything. At the time, I didn't have anything going except the deal I had put together to build Cumberland River. I had already sunk all the money I had into it, and I had to rely on my investors to keep the project going. On paper I looked great but, in reality, it wouldn't have taken much to throw me into bankruptcy. Shelley didn't understand that I didn't have a lot of cash, that I couldn't buy her expensive things, or a new car, or take her on lavish vacations. We wanted different things. Sometimes I think we stayed together because it was convenient.'

Amanda clenched her hands together. Part of her wanted to bolt and run. She had been away from Price for nearly two months and she was just now able to think of him without crying. The other part of her wanted to reach out to him, to touch his cheek and smooth the worried lines in his forehead and tell him that she loved him, that she never wanted to be apart from him again.

'Were you in love with her?' whispered Amanda, wanting so badly to know but afraid to hear the answer.

'I don't know. I thought I was.' His blue eyes took on a faraway look.

Amanda felt her heart contract.

Price paused, then continued. 'Then Shelley told me she was pregnant.'

The room was silent. Amanda squeezed her eyes closed tightly, wanting to shut out what she had just heard. Then she forced herself to look at him, willing him to go on.

She had to know.

Price's voice was carefully controlled. 'One minute I was OK with the idea of being a father, the next I wasn't sure that I was ready for that kind of responsibility. But I didn't have much choice. Shelley was about a month along when she told me. After some soul-searching on my part and a lot of pressure from her, we decided to get married right away. Only our families were present.'

Price's eyes collided with Amanda's. 'Don't even say what you're thinking,' he pleaded, knowing that the circumstances of his marriage to Shelley and then his marriage to her were much too similar for comfort. 'I could have refused to marry her – unmarried women with children are no longer scorned like they were in my parents' generation – but it wasn't the right thing to do.'

'And you always do the right thing,' Amanda said, unable to keep her hurt at bay, then wishing she had remained silent when she saw the pain her words had caused.

Slowly, he shook his head. 'I thought…I don't know what I thought. I wanted to walk away, but I couldn't.'

'How did she feel about the baby?' Amanda asked quietly.

'OK, or so I thought. She surprised me. I never realised she had any maternal instincts, but I figured I'd misjudged her.'

Price wished he knew what Amanda was thinking, but she sat still, watching him, her eyes wide, her normally expressive face carefully composed. Never in his life would he ever be as vulnerable, as exposed, as he was right now. Never would he have as much at stake.

He continued. 'By that time, construction had already begun at the Cumberland site, so our honeymoon was just a long weekend. It wasn't so different from a lot of other weekend trips we had taken. The only real difference was that we were married. Then we both went back to work. I was spending most of my time out of town and, once, when I was able to get home a day earlier than I had planned, I thought I'd surprise Shelley, so I went directly to her office to take her to lunch.' Price stood and began to pace. 'Patty, Shelley's assistant, told me that Shelley had collapsed that morning at work and had been taken to the hospital. I raced to the emergency room. When I arrived, Shelley was already out of surgery and had been moved to a room. Jenny, her sister, was there with her.'

He returned to the chair he had occupied earlier, sat down on the edge and buried his face in his hands. The hurt had faded, but the memory hadn't. His lips thinned into a hard line as he raised his head and continued his narrative.

But his mind wasn't nearly as dispassionate, and the scene that day at the hospital replayed itself vividly...

'How is she?' Price had asked as he rushed into the room.

Jenny looked up. 'Price! I'm so glad you're here. She's going to be OK. It was her appendix. But they operated before it got really bad.'

He went to stand beside Shelley's bed. Against the stark white of the sheets she looked like a ghost, as if all the colour had been drained from her body. Her hair had lost its sheen. Even her lips had a purplish tinge. He leaned over and kissed her on the forehead, but she didn't stir from her anaesthesia-induced slumber.

'Did you know she'd been having reoccurring abdominal pain?' asked Jenny.

Price sighed and shook his head. 'No. I've been out of town, except for a few days here and there, for nearly a month. We talked almost every night, but she didn't mention it. Maybe she didn't want me to worry. I stopped by her office today – Patty was the one who told me she was here. I wasn't supposed to be back in town till tomorrow.'

Just then, there was a brief knock at the door and a nurse came in. 'Mr McCord? Dr Latham, the surgeon who operated on your wife, can talk to you now if you'll come with me.'

Price followed the nurse out of the room and down the hall. When they reached a set of double doors marked 'No Admittance', she stopped.

'He's just coming out of another surgery,' the nurse said. 'If you'll wait here, he'll be right out.'

In less than a minute, the doctor appeared. 'Mr McCord? I'm Dr Latham. Your wife is going to be fine. She had acute appendicitis. There was some infection.

Any surgery carries some risk, of course, but this is a fairly common procedure. I don't expect any complications, although we'll watch her for the next few days. In a couple of weeks, she should be as good as new.'

Price nodded, relieved. 'And the baby – everything's OK with it?' he asked.

The doctor frowned. 'Your wife is pregnant?'

'Yes, two-and-a-half months. You didn't know?'

Dr Latham shook his head. 'No,' he said slowly. 'She was admitted through the emergency room. Let me get her chart. Meanwhile, I'll have the gynaecologist on staff check her, unless you'd rather call in your own doctor.'

'No, no,' said Price. 'The doctor on staff will be fine.'

After the doctor had retreated behind the double doors, Price headed back toward Shelley's room. He walked slowly, more worried now than he had been earlier. What if something had happened to the baby? A sense of dread settled heavily on his shoulders.

'I think I'll go on home now, unless you need me to stay,' Jenny said when Price returned.

He looked up as if he hadn't heard her.

'Price? Is everything OK?' she asked. 'The doctor didn't…'

Oh, no. Everything's OK. Shelley will be back to normal in a few weeks. Thanks, Jenny. You go on home. I'll be here for a while then I may go by the office. I'll come back again this evening. She ought to be awake by then.'

Jenny picked up her bag and her jacket. When she reached the door Price said, 'Uh, Jenny? Were you here when Shelley was in the emergency room?'

'No, I got here about a half-hour later, why?'

'So you didn't fill out the admission forms for her?'

'No. Is something wrong?'

'Everything's fine. I was just wondering, that's all.'

Jenny smiled. 'When she wakes up, tell her I'll be back to see her tomorrow.'

Price sat down in the chair next to Shelley's bed and took hold of her hand. For the first time in a long while he prayed – for his wife and his unborn child.

Two hours later, the obstetrician who had examined Shelley met with Price. 'Let's walk down the hall,' he said.

'Mr McCord, how far along in her pregnancy did you say your wife was?'

'Two-and-a-half months.'

'Has she seen a doctor?'

'She consulted a doctor early, when she first found out she was pregnant, then she had another check-up two weeks ago.'

The doctor shook his head as he studied the clipboard in his hand. 'There's nothing on this admission form that indicates she's pregnant, and the form was signed by your wife.'

'Maybe she wasn't thinking clearly, she must have been in a lot of pain when she arrived.'

I considered that, so I ordered a pregnancy test, just to be sure. The doctor raised his head and looked directly at Price. 'I'm sorry, Mr McCord. Your wife is not pregnant.'

Price broke out in a cold sweat, certain he was about to be sick. He leaned against the wall. He had no idea how long he remained there after the doctor had left, but he knew he couldn't return to Shelley's room just yet. He stopped a passing nurse and got directions to the cafeteria. It was nearly empty since it was already early evening. The coffee from the big stainless steel urn tasted burnt and bitter, but it didn't matter.

He sat at a table near a window that looked out on a small courtyard area. How could this happen? Had Shelley made a mistake? Or had she simply lied? A mistake was something he might be able to live with. But if it was a mistake, then why didn't she say so? And why go through the pretence of seeing the doctor again? A lie, though, was an entirely different matter.

Later, when he returned to her room, Shelley was awake.

'Hi,' she said. She was still groggy, and her speech was slow. 'When did you get home?' She held out her hand to him.

Price went to stand next to her and took her outstretched hand in his. It felt cold. 'A little before eleven. I went to your office. I was going to take you to lunch, but it seems you had other plans.' Even to his own ears, his words were infused with a false cheerfulness. He wondered if she could hear it also. 'I'm sorry I wasn't here to be with you. You should have told me you were having problems.'

'I didn't want to worry you,' she said. Her eyes closed again.

Intermittently, she would wake up and talk to him then drift off. He wanted to ask her the one question that was uppermost in his mind, but he knew it would be unfair. He had to wait until she was home and fully recovered. Until she brought it up.

'I'm getting fat, don't you think?' Shelly asked, studying her profile in the mirror. She had been out of the hospital for nearly two weeks and would soon be going back to work.

Price took a deep breath. This was it. He had waited, biding his time until the moment was right. 'You look exactly the same size to me,' he said.

'No, I've definitely gained weight. The doctor said...'

'What did he say, Shelley?' The question was sharp, the cynicism clear.

She didn't turn, but her eyes met his in the mirror.

'How long did you think you could carry out this charade?'

'What are you talking about? Can't you see?' She arched her back slightly, creating a rounded bulge where there was none, then slowly smoothed her hand over it.

'Stop it, Shelley. I know that you're not pregnant. It was all a scheme, wasn't it? Just to get me to marry you.'

She dropped her hand and turned to face him.

'On the admission forms, you forgot to tell the hospital you were pregnant and, after your surgery, when I asked if the baby was OK, the doctor said that there was nothing on your chart about you being pregnant.'

She shrugged. 'It was an oversight.'

'It was a lie.'

'How did you find out?'

'They did a pregnancy test.'

Shelley came up to him then she reached out and wrapped her arms around his neck. 'Well, now you know. It will be so much nicer without a baby to tie us down. I'm really not cut out for motherhood anyway. But I did want you, Price – and now I have you.'

Amanda watched him, her heart breaking as he told her what was obviously a very painful story. It took all her control to remain where she was and hear him out. 'What did you do then?' she asked softly.

Price dropped his head in his hands for a moment and then looked up and focused once more on Amanda. 'Her voice was so cold and callous. I remember how unimportant she made it all sound, how unemotional she was.'

'Oh, Price,' whispered Amanda as her hands went to her lips.

He leaned his head back against the chair. His hands gripped the arms. 'I just couldn't understand why Shelley would do something so deceitful. It was as if I had married a stranger. She had turned into someone I didn't know, someone I loathed. I left then and drove around for hours. In the space of one afternoon, my life had come apart. I felt cheated and betrayed. I swore then that I would never let another woman get that close to me.'

He took a deep breath, then stood and walked towards the window. 'By the end of the following day, I had filed for an annulment. The marriage had lasted two months.'

He went to Amanda, taking her hands in his and pulling her to her feet. 'Can you understand now why I didn't tell you about this?' He reached out for her, but she stepped out of his reach.

'Because of the baby,' Amanda answered, her voice curiously flat. 'You married me so you would have a child.'

He cursed and gathered her into his arms. 'The reason I wanted to marry you, honey, is because I love you. I knew you would never do what Shelley had done. You would want this child with me or without me.'

Price pulled back to look at her. His eyes were dark and turbulent. 'We've had a stormy relationship right from the very beginning, but the one thing you have to believe is that I love you. I don't want to be without you ever again, but I can if you force me to. It's time for you to make your choice, Amanda.'

Love shouldn't be this complicated.

His hands moved up and down her arms. He couldn't get enough of her. All he really wanted to do was make love to her, to show her what she meant to him. But he waited for her answer.

The feel of his hands on her brought back memories. They were strong, masculine hands capable of doing incredible things to her. She looked away quickly. Thoughts of their love-making seemed almost indecent.

'I need some time,' she said breathlessly.

'No,' he said, his voice unyielding. 'You've had your time. Two months of it. Two months that I've missed waking up next to you each morning. Two months when we should have been loving our baby daughter together.'

'Price, maybe we shouldn't rush this,' said Amanda, her voice pleading.

'Rush this?' Price said. 'Who do you think you're talking to? I'm not some stranger that you can politely put off until it's convenient for you. I know I caused all this, but this has been hell for me, Amanda. I'm the man who made love to you, who taught you how to love in return. Remember how we made love, Amanda?'

His eyes had turned a dark murky blue and they sliced through her like white hot steel, forcing her to remember things she had managed to put aside. Until tonight.

'Please, let me go,' said Amanda, scared of the intensity of her desire.

'No,' answered Price. 'Not unless you can tell me with absolute certainty that you don't love me.' His blue eyes were stormy, his dark hair fell carelessly on to his forehead. He leaned toward her and his lips found hers. His arms surrounded her as his hands reached down to mould her body to his. His tongue probed insistently, coaxing and parting her lips.

It was there, that immediate flash of heat that started low in her stomach and raced throughout her body. How could she say she didn't love this man with all her heart? She trembled, then surrendered – realising it was inevitable.

'I've missed you so much. I wish I had handled things differently from the beginning, but now I've got to know if you love me enough to start again,' said Price, his voice husky.

From the first summer she had met him, from the day he had appeared at her door, from the first time he had made love to her, from the moment she had walked into her apartment earlier this evening and saw him giving Meg her bottle, Amanda knew that no matter how much she tried, she would never be complete without this man.

Her eyes were bright with unshed tears when she looked up at him and whispered the words that had always been in her heart. 'I have never loved anyone but you,' she said, 'and I never will.'

Suddenly, it was all so simple.

Forthcoming titles from HEARTLINE:

OPPOSITES ATTRACT by Kay Gregory
Although *he* doesn't realise it, Venetia Quinn has been in love with her boss, Caleb, ever since he hired her. To Caleb, she's just one of the boys...but a passion filled night has consequences which neither of them could have anticipated...

DECEPTION by June Ann Monks
As a result of his childhood, Ben has always taken a serious approach to life, so 'Kathy Lam's' arrival – she faints in his arms – makes him realise what he's been missing. 'Kathy' has loved Ben all of her life, but what will happen when he discovers that she's been deceiving him?

TROUBLE AT THE TOP by Louise Armstrong
Highly ambitions and fast-moving Nikki has been appointed to close down a once successful business. The one man who stands in her way is gorgeous and sexy Alexander Davidson...definitely a force to be reckoned with!

APPLES FOR THE TEACHER by Steffi Gerrard
Ellie is an experienced teacher of adults, but finds it incredibly difficult to cope with Chris Martin – the most extraordinary handsome and sexy man she's ever met. In fact, it is isn't longer before Ellie is beginning to wonder if Chris Martin is all that he seems.

Why not start a new romance today with Heartline Books. We will send you an exciting Heartline romance ABSOLUTELY FREE. You can then discover the benefits of our home delivery service: Heartline Books Direct.

Each month, before they reach the shops, you will receive four brand new titles, delivered directly to your door.

All you need to do, is to fill in your details opposite – and return them to us at the Freepost address.

Please send me my free book:

Name (IN BLOCK CAPITALS)

_____

Address (IN BLOCK CAPITALS)

_____

_____

_____

_____ Postcode _____

Address:
HEARTLINE BOOKS
FREEPOST LON 16243,
Swindon SN2 8LA

We may use this information to send you offers from ourselves or selected companies, which may be of interest to you.

If you do not wish to receive further offers
from Heartline Books, please tick this box ☐

If you do not wish to receive further offers
from other companies, please tick this box ☐

Once you receive your free book, unless we hear from you otherwise, within fourteen days, we will be sending you four exciting new romantic novels at a price of £3.99 each, plus £1 p&p. Thereafter, each time you buy our books, we will send you a further pack of four titles.

You can cancel at any time! You have no obligation to ever buy a single book.

Heartline Books – romance at its best!

What do you think of this month's selection?

As we are determined to continue to offer you books which are up to the high standard we know you expect from Heartline, we need you to tell us about *your* reading likes and dislikes. So can we please ask you to spare a few moments to fill in the questionnaire on the following pages and send it back to us? And don't be shy – if you wish to send in a form for each title you have read this month, we'll be delighted to hear from you!

Questionnaire

Please tick the boxes to indicate your answers:

1 Did you enjoy reading this Heartline book?

   Title of book: _____

   A lot   ☐
   A little   ☐
   Not at all   ☐

2 What did you particularly like about this book?

   Believable characters ☐
   Easy to read   ☐
   Enjoyable locations   ☐
   Interesting story   ☐
   Good value for money   ☐
   Favourite author   ☐
   Modern setting   ☐

3 If you didn't like this book, can you please tell us why?

   _____
   _____

4 Would you buy more Heartline Books each month if they were available?

Yes ☐
No – four is enough ☐

5 What other kinds of books do you enjoy reading?

Historical fiction ☐
Puzzle books ☐
Crime/Detective fiction ☐
Non-fiction ☐
Cookery books ☐

Other _____

_____

6 Which magazines and/or newspapers do you read regularly?

a) _____

b) _____

c) _____

d) _____

And now a bit about you:

Name _____

Address _____

_____

_____ Postcode _____

Thank you so much for completing this questionnaire.
Now just tear it out and send it in an envelope to:

HEARTLINE BOOKS
PO Box 400
Swindon SN2 6EJ

(and if you don't want to spoil this book, please feel free
to write to us at the above address with your comments
and opinions.)

Code: JFON

Have you missed any of the following books:

The Windrush Affairs *by Maxine Barry*
Soul Whispers *by Julia Wild*
Beguiled *by Kay Gregory*
Red Hot Lover *by Lucy Merritt*
Stay Very Close *by Angela Drake*
Jack of Hearts *by Emma Carter*
Destiny's Echo *by Julie Garrett*
The Truth Game *by Margaret Callaghan*
His Brother's Keeper *by Kathryn Bellamy*
Never Say Goodbye *by Clare Tyler*
Fire Storm *by Patricia Wilson*
Altered Images *by Maxine Barry*
Second Time Around *by June Ann Monks*
Running for Cover *by Harriet Wilson*
Yesterday's Man *by Natalie Fox*
Moth to the Flame *by Maxine Barry*
Dark Obsession *by Lisa Andrews*
Once Bitten…Twice Shy *by Sue Dukes*
Shadows of the Past *by Elizabeth Forsyth*
Perfect Partners *by Emma Carter*
Melting the Iceman *by Maxine Barry*
Marrying A Stranger *by Sophie Jaye*
Secrets *by Julia Wild*
Special Delivery *by June Ann Monks*
Bittersweet Memories *by Carole Somerville*
Hidden Dreams *by Jean Drew*
The Peacock House *by Clare Tyler*
Crescendo *by Patricia Wilson*
The Wrong Bride *by Susanna Carr*
Forbidden *by Megan Paul*
Playing with Fire *by Kathryn Bellamy*
Collision Course *by Joyce Halliday*
Illusions *by Julia Wild*
It Had To Be You *by Lucy Merritt*
Summer Magic *by Ann Bruce*
Imposters In Paradise *by Maxine Barry*

Complete your collection by ringing the Heartline Hotline on 0845 6000504, visiting our website <u>www.heartlinebooks.com</u> or writing to us at Heartline Books, PO Box 400, Swindon SN2 6EJ